e Hideout

unting

I0956143

A TRUMPET CLUB SPECIAL EDITION

Published by The Trumpet Club
666 Fifth Avenue, New York, New York 10103

ISBN 0-440-84580-7

This edition published by arrangement with
Harcourt Brace Jovanovich, Inc.
Designed by Camilla Filancia
Cover illustration by Greg Shed
Printed in the United States of America
January 1992

10 9 8 7 6 5 4 3 2 1
OPM

With love to
Lara and Ken Clardy,
who know everything
and share.

The Hideout

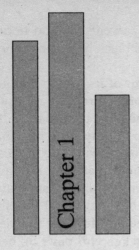

Chapter 1

When I found the key marked *T* I thought it was the best thing that had ever happened to me. But it didn't turn out to be.

I was sitting on a wall by the Countess International Hotel in San Francisco, my hand closed tightly around the forty-five stolen dollars in my pocket, wondering what to do next. I knew I couldn't just sit there forever, watching the flurry of tourists, the bellmen in their gray uniforms who clustered in the hotel entrance under its silver-and-gray-striped awning. Not that anybody was paying any attention to me. I was just a kid, a boy in jeans and a Forty Niners sweatshirt, hanging out. But I'd been there long enough. I had to make plans. I had to stop feeling so lost and alone.

It was hot, even though it was only eleven o'clock

in the morning. I took off my sweatshirt and tied it around my waist, watching the black limousines lined head to tail along the curb.

One was pulling silently out of its row to double-park directly in front of the hotel entrance, and I saw a lady with silvery white hair heading toward it, walking slowly down the long strip of gray carpeting that led from the front door. She was carrying one of those oval-shaped little cases that hold makeup and have a mirror on the lid. My mom has one. Paul Paws bought it for her on her last birthday. Paul Paws! I call him that because since he and Mom got married two years ago he can't seem to keep his paws off her. Like when he gave her the makeup case, saying, "I had the saleslady put some stuff in there. I told her it was for a gorgeous, tawny-haired woman with great, green cat's eyes who just happens to be my wife." He was rubbing her neck, his gold wedding ring glinting in the sun. He and she have identical rings except that his is engraved *I'm Yours* and hers *You're Mine*, or maybe it's the other way around. Paul Paws makes me sick to my stomach.

The white-haired lady from the hotel reached the limousine. Behind her was a little man, probably her husband, carrying a black poodle with a diamond collar. I guess they were real diamonds if the dog was a guest at the Countess International. Behind them was a gray-uniformed bellman pushing a metal luggage cart; behind him was the doorman, so important

2

looking, rushing to open the door of the limo which the chauffeur was already rushing to open, too. I had a glimpse of the inside of the car as the lady stepped on board: dark velvet seats, a rose in a silver vase, a telephone, a TV set.

The husband and the driver and the doorman all supervised the loading of the luggage. The doorman got to hold the dog while the husband stepped in beside his wife, and the poodle growled real growls and aimed his sharp little teeth at the doorman's nose.

"Good doggie," the doorman kept saying, jerking his head back out of reach. "Nice doggie." Right in the middle of all that, the little man leaned out the car door, exchanged the dog for a big wad of money and something small and shiny that looked like a key.

"Thank you, sir. Thank you very much." As the doorman struggled to get the money into his pocket and hand over the dog, the key fell soundlessly onto the gray carpet.

The limo moved away. The bellman was talking to the doorman, gesturing toward the pocket that held the money. The doorman was shrugging and shaking his head.

"Thanks for my share, Murphy!" the bellman said in a disgusted voice louder than it should have been.

The key lay where it had fallen.

I slipped off the wall and began moving casually in that direction. That key might come in useful.

A group of tourists had come out of the hotel and

were standing together on the gray carpet. I strolled behind them. One of them had the toe of his black shoe right on top of the key. I passed them by, turned.

The one with his foot on the key was pointing toward the bank near the little park across the street. As he took a step forward, I swooped, grabbed the key, and slid it into my pocket.

Walking away from the hotel, I kept expecting to hear a yell behind me . . . "Hey, kid! Boy! I saw you pick up that key. Bring it back here!"

But nobody yelled anything.

I hurried another half block before I let myself stop and examine what I had. It looked like a regular house key except that it was big, and square on top. I guessed it had to be for one of the hotel rooms, or why would the guy have given it to the doorman? It was probably for the room they'd been staying in, and the rich guest had forgotten it till the last minute. The letter *T* was engraved on the square head.

Shouldn't there be a number on here, a room number? Four years ago, when Mom and I stayed in that motel in Santa Rosa, we had a key with 263 on it. We'd had a good time in Santa Rosa. That was BPP and AD: Before Paul Paws and After Dad. I think that was maybe the last good time Mom and I'd had together.

Could be they didn't put numbers on the keys of the Countess in case one got lost and a thief found it. Well, a thief *had* found it. The minute I took that money from Paul Paws I'd qualified myself, hadn't I? But maybe taking from your stepdad doesn't count. Anyway, my real dad would refund it to him—with interest.

Could *T* mean third floor? Tenth? Twentieth? I stared up at the hotel. Crikes, the place could be thirty floors high, especially in that tallest part. I thought it was a pretty ugly hotel, actually, even though the *Chronicle* has written about how some famous architect built it, and how it's a perfect example of this and that. To me it looked like a bundle of glass tubes, all different heights, glued together and standing on their ends with little scoops of balconies, curved windows that mirrored the sun, and glass elevators crawling up on the outside like bugs.

I stared again at the key. Now that I had it, what was I going to do with it? Suppose I turned it in? Would there be a reward? I doubted it. Maybe I should try giving it to Murphy, the important doorman. Maybe he'd be so grateful he'd fork over some cash. No way. That Murphy was a tightwad.

Suppose I tried to find the room? I was getting hungry—isn't there always a refrigerator filled with food in expensive hotel rooms? You see that all the time on TV. The motel in Santa Rosa hadn't had anything except a Coke machine in the hall and an ice maker that made only water. But this would be different. The thought of food made my stomach growl. If I'd been smarter this morning, I'd have

5

grabbed some stuff from our dark kitchen, some fruit or a little box of cereal. Something. But after taking the money I'd been in too much of a hurry to get away. I'd been sweating real sweat. Remembering the way I'd gone through Paul Paws's wallet made me sweat again.

I'd crept into their room, sun already coming through the gap where the drapes don't quite meet in the middle, holding my breath as I tiptoed past the bed where Paul Paws lay with one muscly arm thrown across my mom. Her face was buried in the pillow, her hair all tangled the way it is in the morning, all through breakfast; most of the time she doesn't bother to comb it till after she's had her shower.

"You look like a wanton," Paul Paws said one morning. "I love your hair like that." I'd looked up *wanton* in the dictionary later, and I don't think Mom looks like a wanton at all. I guess her hair is tawny, though. I'd looked that up, too. Her hair's dark brown with stripes of gold, like a tiger's coat. She says when I was little, mine was that color, too. But it darkened.

"It's like your dad's now," Mom said once. "Twelve years old and everything about you like your dad, even your ears." I thought she'd sounded sad.

Looking down at her this morning as I was leaving, all I could see was that tangle of tawny hair. I was half wishing she would turn so I could see her face for the last time when, suddenly, Paul Paws moved. He grunted and rolled on his back, and I froze, waiting for his breathing to even out again. He got back into his snore, the ends of his black mustache quivering.

His wallet was on the dresser. I eased it off and pulled out the bills, all of them. The folded money felt thick and comforting. I didn't dare count it till I was downstairs. Forty-five dollars. It had felt like more, but there were a lot of singles. It would have to do. Do for what? To get me where I was going? No way would it get me where I was going, because I was going to England, to my dad. But it would help. I'd opened the back door and shut it gently behind me.

Skeeter, the dog next door, barked, recognized me, and began jumping happily at the gate. I'm his only friend. I'm the only one who walks him or talks to him. Nobody in that house bothers.

For a minute I thought about taking him with me. A boy and his dog! But it would be hard enough to get to London myself. They probably wouldn't let a big old raggedy mutt like Skeeter come.

I headed for downtown, walking. One good thing about San Francisco is you can walk just about any-where if you don't mind hills. You can take a cable car real easy and cheap, too, but I didn't want to spend anything if I could help it.

I'd been sitting on the wall by the Countess In-

ternational considering my situation when the doorman dropped the key. Now I was standing, looking
down at it shining and silver in the palm of my hand.
I decided to find the door the key fit and see what
happened. If it was to a room, I'd have a place to
spend the night. At least now I had the beginning of
a plan.

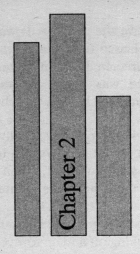

Chapter 2

I didn't walk along that path of pale gray carpet that led to the Countess International front entrance. Instead I went around the side on the paving stones and pushed open the curved glass doors that had *C.I.* on them in gold.

The lobby was huge, with more of that thick gray carpeting. Flowers and ferns in big pots trailed down white pedestals. People lounged in gray-and-pink-striped armchairs or stood around talking or waited in line at a shiny counter, long as the Great Wall of China. Nobody paid any attention to me. They probably thought I was just somebody's kid. Well, I was. There were lots of kids around, mostly standing with their parents, though. Had they missed me yet at home? Probably not. It was Saturday, and on Saturdays Mom and Paul Paws sleep late.

I glanced at the clocks above the counter. It was hard to find one with San Francisco time, since they had everybody's time up there. In London it was seven-thirty at night. If Dad was home he was probably watching the telly, which is what he calls TV.

"I hope you're not watching too much telly, Andy. It rots the brain." That's what he'd written to me once and I'd heard Mom say to Paul Paws, "Don't you love the way he worries about his son's mental health?"

Of course, Dad might not be home. He's an archaeologist, and he's been working off and on forever at this dig in the Thames Valley. He comes and goes. One time, I guess it was six years ago, he went and never came back. "He always liked England better," Mom told me. "After all, he was born there."

"It's not because he doesn't like us, is it?" I'd asked.

"Of course not. Certainly not because he doesn't like you."

It was eleven-thirty in the morning San Francisco time. Mom would for sure have missed me by now. She'd probably called up the stairs, "Andy? Andy . . ."

"Sir? Young man?" That wasn't Mom calling. My heart swung like a pendulum as I glanced over my shoulder.

A guy behind the shining counter was pointing at

10

me. He wore the same uniform all the desk people were wearing. Gray tuxedo jacket with a white starched front and a gray-and-silver-striped tie. The gleaming gold plate above the desk said Assistant Manager.

I took another step, as if I hadn't heard him and he called again, louder this time. "Young man?"

I stopped, looked all around, and then pointed to myself as if to say, "Are you talking to me?" I guess I'd stuck on a smile, too, because I could feel my face stretch out. Inside me that pendulum was still swinging like crazy. Should I turn and run? I could be out of there before that bozo could jump over the desk.

He signaled for me to come closer.

I took a step toward him, then stopped again.

He leaned forward, examining me carefully through gold-rimmed glasses, probably trying to remember if he'd seen me check in with rich important parents or if I was just some low-life who'd wandered in from the street.

"Are you a registered guest in our hotel, sir?" His voice was polite, but sharp enough so that a couple of people turned to look.

I fished in my pocket and held up the key with my thumb over the *T* on the square end. It was as if I'd produced a magic wand that could turn a frog into a prince.

"I see. Thank you very much, sir." He was smiling

now and stroking the top of his balding head. "Have a nice day, sir."

I let out my breath and started walking again, the key slippery in my hand. Oh, man! Suppose he'd come all the way around that desk and asked for my name and checked it on his computer or whatever they use to see if someone is for real. I peered secretively in all directions. Where were the elevators?

I walked past a dress shop with a fur cape in the window and a fox stuffed so well he could have been real, past a candy shop with a single box of candy and one red rose in the window. It was a safe bet they didn't sell Snickers bars in there.

Where *were* the elevators?

And then I saw them, the curved gray doors, the lighted squares on the side that you push to go up or down.

Five people were waiting so I stood beside them staring straight ahead, my hands stuffed in my pockets.

"I saw your team play the Rams last year," the man next to me said.

It took a couple of seconds for me to realize he was talking to me. I glanced up at him nervously.

"The Forty Niners!" He prodded the back of the bunched-up sweatshirt I'd tied at my waist. I guess the logo still showed.

"That Candlestick is sure some windy ballpark," he said.

I nodded, looking up sideways at the panels that told where the elevators were, checking them all the way across. Two were going up. One was on the second floor. Hurry and come down, I thought. Get a move on.

"I'm a Saints fan myself," the man said, and the lady with him rolled her eyes and said, "Is he *ever*." The guy began to tap one foot and hum "When the Saints Go Marching In."

The lady smiled down at me. She had the blackest hair I'd ever seen, held up on top with a silver needle thing.

"Are you vacationing?" the lady asked. "We're from New Orleans."

I was about to say, "No, I live in San Francisco," but I stopped in time. And just then a polite little chime sounded and the elevator doors slid open. Thank goodness.

We all stepped into the curved glass box, and immediately people began pushing floor buttons.

"Which one for you, son?" the Saints man asked.

The numbers on the panels went up to thirty. No button said *T*. I'd start at the top and work my way down. Maybe I'd get lucky. *T* might even *be* thirty.

"Thirty," I said.

The lady beamed.

"Why, that's our floor, too. We must be neighbors."

"We must be," I said and turned a little so I

wouldn't have to talk anymore. Next she'd be asking me my room number.

It was the strangest thing going straight up in that see-through elevator, the tubes of the Countess International reflecting each other and us, the city buildings below, the cars and trucks, the orange curve of the Golden Gate Bridge, Alcatraz, and sailboat sails fluttering, white as sea gulls.

I knew the elevator had been stopping and starting, but by the time I turned to look there were only the three of us left, me and the Saints. Bad luck that we'd all be getting off together. What if this nice lady stopped and watched to see that I made it safely to my room? She looked the type.

Quickly I pushed twenty-nine.

"Changed your mind?" she asked.

"I forgot," I said. "I was thinking thirty. But thirty's wrong."

"You're not lost now, are you?" She had the nicest, softest voice. For a second I thought I was going to bawl because of the way she said that. And because I *was* lost. Sort of.

"It's such a big hotel," she added, and I could tell she was afraid she'd insulted me, made me sound babyish.

I pulled the key from my pocket, keeping my thumb over the *T* part again.

"Well, I see you're all right." She touched her husband's shoulder. "Doug? You remembered *our* key, didn't you?"

The guy slipped it out of the pocket of his white jacket and balanced it on his hand. Plain as plain I saw the number on the square head—3009. But where was the number on mine? What was it with this *T* thing?

We were stopping now at twenty-nine, the doors gliding open.

"Hope we see you again," the lady said. "But I suppose it's not likely. We leave tomorrow. By the way, we forgot to ask your name?"

I kept the doors from closing with my shoulder. "Andy," I said. "Bye."

I waited till the elevator hissed upward before I started along the corridor. My feet made no sound on the thick rug. There was no one around and the silence was as deep as the silence in an empty church. The doors were marked 2902, 2904. Even numbers on the left, odd on the right. Lots of the doorknobs had Do Not Disturb signs hung on them. Trays, politely covered with cloth napkins, sat outside some of the rooms. When I lifted one napkin I found two blueberry muffins in a basket. I stuffed one in each pocket and told myself that taking the money might have been stealing but this was called Not Wasting Good Food. No need to think I was being a thief again.

At the end of the corridor was a huge curved window with a view across the city and two doors, one marked Private, the other marked Stairs. Nothing at all that said *T*. The private room was filled

15

with housekeeping supplies—rags, mops, dustpans, rubber gloves—and the stairs were cement and uncarpeted. I went up them, cramming the muffins in my mouth as I went. Man, was I starved!

The thirtieth floor was exactly like the twenty-ninth. I passed 3009, and for some reason knowing the Saints were there made me feel better. Then I took the stairs all the way down, looking along the twentieth floors, the twelfth, tenth, second. Maids in gray uniforms pushed cleaning carts soundlessly along the carpeted corridors, spoke to each other in hushed voices. Through open doors, I saw sheets being whisked off beds, heard the low hum of vacuum cleaners. No *T* room.

"You can come stay with us," my friend Leah had said once before when I'd told her I was going to split. That time I'd chickened out.

"Come to my place," she'd said.

"Oh, sure. And two minutes after I get there your mom would be calling my mom. Moms stick together." Besides, our mothers have been friends forever.

"My mom doesn't have to know," Leah had said. "I'll hide you."

"Where?" I asked.

Leah's apartment has three of the tiniest bedrooms in the whole world. Hers is jam-packed with her ham radio stuff. You couldn't squeeze a cockroach into that room. Her parents and her little brother, Parker, are in the other two.

"You can always find a place to hide if you try," Leah said. "The cellar, or the garage, or . . ."

"You don't have a cellar," I'd said. "And your garage is a carport. I'd be a dweeb to hide in a carport."

But Leah's apartment was beginning to sound better all the time, since I'd now checked all the floors and found nothing. I figured I knew this hotel so well I could have drawn a map of it. I decided *T* wasn't a room at all; it was something I couldn't even begin to imagine. It would have been nice if I could have found it, though, just for this one night. Because thinking about night coming, and the dark, and being alone, and having nowhere to go made my stomach collapse. What do runaways do at night? I could sleep in that little park across the street. Or in the BART station. Would they let you? Maybe you'd have to find a doorway, and it would be cold because it's always cold in San Francisco at night with the wind coming in off the bay and the fog drifting white and wet along the sidewalks. Even that old guy who sings about San Francisco sings about the fog. And there'd be crazies hanging around: crack dealers, druggies, street people who push their belongings in shopping carts and who ask for money and sometimes try to talk loony talk to you. Oh, man! Could I get a room with Paul Paws's forty-five bucks and the twelve dollars I had of my own? Not in this hotel, for sure, but somewhere? I could go home, of course, say "Mom, I'm back."

17

No. Never. I'd never go back. Not after what she'd said. I'd sleep in a doorway first.

One of the elevators was waiting. I'd ride down. Down and out. I stepped in and stared through the glass walls. Hey! Wait a sec! This hotel has all those mirrored tubes, and I'd only tried one of them. Shoot, there were four others. That had to be it. "*T*'s in another tube, you dummy," I said out loud. "Just go check the rest of them."

One thing I will say for myself, I can get my optimism back pretty fast. To get to the smaller lobby I had to walk through the main lobby again, along a curved passageway where plants climbed up the walls even though it was indoors, where a waterfall splashed and big yellow fish swam under a real bridge.

Paul Paws would like this place. He's a landscape designer, which is another way of saying he's a fancy gardener, so he's interested in this kind of stuff.

This time I found the elevators fast. Four guys got off the first one that arrived, and I slipped into the glass sun-filled emptiness they left behind. The lighted number panel was right in front of me. Thirty-four floors in this tube. I stared at the panel, and then my heart began doing that swinging thing again as I saw the small, brass circle directly above the number thirty-four. On it was the single letter *T*.

Below the *T* was a small keyhole.

My hand shook as I reached up and touched it, as I took out the *T* key and tried it in the lock. It was a perfect fit.

18

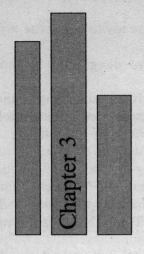

Chapter 3

When I turned the key, the elevator began rising, fast as an express train on its way to heaven.

Above the doors, the lighted panels flashed, floor numbers zooming past at a sickening speed. My ears popped. Thirty-four, and blankness, and then the small *T* inside the brass button glowed red and the elevator stopped. The doors slid open. On the wall directly opposite was a small gold plate engraved with the words Tower Suite. *T* for Tower. *That's* what it was. But what was it? My heart fluttered as I stepped out into a small lobby, white-carpeted with white-and-silver walls. There was a marble slab of a table. A humungous vase filled with tall pink flowers was reflected in a big, silver-framed mirror. I could see myself in the mirror, too, my face pale and frightened. I saw myself crouched, ready to run at the first hint of danger.

But there was no hint of danger, no sound, nothing.

Two gray doors to the left and the right of the mirror were both closed and the silence and the smell of the flowers was somehow creepy. It felt like a funeral place. What if I opened one of those doors and there was a dead person lying in a coffin? Maybe if a guest died this was where they brought him. They'd lay him out first on that slab of a table with the flowers at his feet. *T* for Tomb. No, bozo. Stop it. *T* was for Tower Suite.

Behind me the doors of the elevator sighed closed. I swung around. Trapped. No. There was a button on the wall with a lock underneath. I'd just have to put in the key and push the square to bring the elevator back. There was a door beside it, white and inconspicuous. I pushed it open. Stairs led down. Good, another way out.

I peered around. Something told me there was nobody here. I tiptoed to the first door and eased it open. The room was empty. It was the fanciest room I'd ever seen, all silver-gray and white with glass that curved around to a view that could pop out your eyeballs. A big black telescope stood on a swivel stand by one of the windows, in case your eyes couldn't handle the view by themselves. There were two white couches and between them a glass table big enough to play Ping-Pong on. A gigantic bowl of fruit stood on the table, next to neatly arranged newspapers and magazines. I tiptoed over to a huge cabinet with carved doors. Behind the doors was the biggest TV screen I'd ever seen, and below it was the refrigerator and freezer, the carved wood in the front disguising it, too. Man, was it stocked. But right away I knew I wouldn't dare take anything. It was packed so neatly there'd be a gap as obvious as a missing tooth.

I went soundlessly back into the lobby and tried the other door.

Behind it was a bedroom, the carpeting soft and white as the fake snow we drape around our fake Christmas tree every year. The bed was shaped like a giant open clamshell. The top, curved and transparent, was the canopy. What if you were lying in that bed and the clam began to close? You could watch yourself being eaten alive because there were mirrors everywhere. I kept meeting myself in them, scaring myself.

Through an open door I got a glimpse of a bathroom with a sunken tub and a mountain of pink towels. Mom would go crazy in there. She'd fill the tub and pour in oil from one of those big bottles and not come out for a week, and Paul Paws would knock on the door and whisper, "It's me, sweetheart," and she'd say, "Just a minute, love," and get out of the bath and wrap herself in a towel and open the door and let him in. I'd heard that happen once, and it made me feel weird, thinking of my mom and Paul Paws in there, and her with no clothes on, but that was dumb because . . .

I froze. Was that the elevator chime?

Oh, criminy! Someone was coming. Voices, now—a woman's and a man's.

I ran for the clamshell bed and squirmed beneath it. Just in time! From under the bed I could see two pairs of shoes, the woman's white and chunky, the man's black and pointed, his pants blue denim. He was pulling a big vacuum with a snakelike hose and carrying a bucket.

"Wow," he said. "I haven't been up here before. Some place! I can't figure them letting anybody bring in a *dog*." By his voice I could tell he was younger than Dad, younger than Paul Paws.

"Honey, when you're that rich, who's going to stop you?" the woman asked. "Besides, that Mr. Tolliver who was here is a bank president. His poodle probably has its own savings account. That's how come it can pee on the Countess carpet." She laughed a deep gurgle of a laugh.

"So where's the spot, Mamie?" the guy asked.

"Spots, honey. We've got four of them. And the bottom of the drape, too."

The black shoes stepped forward and the toe of one traced a circle on the rug. "Dog pee's the worst."

"Uh uh, honey. Once we had a gentleman staying

22

here, one of those show business people, and he brought his chimpanzee. Think yourself lucky this was only a dog."

The guy grunted. From my narrow space under the bed, I saw him throw a piece of gray carpeting on the rug, set the plastic bucket on top. I saw his blue denim knees as he knelt, I saw the soles of his shoes. He took a plastic bag from the bucket and pulled out a small brush, a jar of something, and some pieces of toweling.

"I'll leave you to it, Fred," Mamie said.

"This stuff's not going to come out easy, you know," Fred said, grumpy as could be. "Might have to come back tomorrow." His hands paused in the act of unscrewing the lid from the jar. "How do I get down from this tower place anyway?"

"There's a door beside the elevator. There are stairs. Take them to the thirty-fourth floor and pick up the elevator there."

"C'mon, Mamie. Have a heart. Lugging this thing?" He kicked back toward the vacuum. "It weighs a ton."

"OK. Here, take my key. I'll be on the third floor, Freddy. You stop off on the way down and give it back to me, hear? I'll bring you up again tomorrow if you have to come. I change the fruit and the papers and flowers first thing anyway."

Fred sat back on his heels. "How come? Nobody hardly uses this place. Two or three times a year it gets taken. That's what Pat Fitzgerald on the desk told me."

"We keep it ready, just in case, that's how come."

Fred gave his bad-tempered grunt. "Got to keep the rich bums happy, huh?"

The white shoes headed toward the door. "Bring the key, Fred, and get the elevator for me."

I saw him stand. "I was thinking," he said. "If there's stairs, what's the need for this special key business? Anybody could come up."

"Uh uh. The stair doors push only from this direction. It's a fire requirement."

Their voices grew fainter.

I eased my legs. One of them had cramped. I wished to heck Mamie and Fred would both leave so I could get out of here.

There was the faint chime of the elevator, and then Fred was back, prowling around, not going near the poodle spots on the rug. He kicked the edge of the drape. "Stupid dog!" He paced some more, and when he stopped I guessed he was looking at himself in one of the mirrors. I couldn't see his face but I imagined it, long and pointy like his feet, bad-tempered like his voice. I imagined a ratty chin.

Drawers opened and closed. He went out on the balcony.

My leg had cramped again but I was afraid to stretch it. What if he saw a foot sticking out from under the bed and he grabbed and pulled and there I'd be, squirming like a fish on a line?

24

He was coming back. I almost had a heart attack when he walked straight over to the bed and threw himself on it. It bounced, bumping my head. The bouncing eased and everything was quiet—except for my heart, which was still bouncing about on its own.

"I guess I'd better not leave this stuff around," Fred said, and for an awful minute I thought he was talking to me.

He stood and I watched his feet walk across, watched him jam the cleaning stuff and the piece of carpeting into the bucket, grab the vacuum hose, and head back toward the bed. Oh, no! He lifted the edge of the pink cover and tried to shove everything underneath. But the bucket was too tall. So was the vacuum.

Suppose he bent down and tried to force them and saw me . . . But he didn't. He gave that grunt I was beginning to know and walked across to the closet, the vacuum trailing behind him like a dog on a leash. He rolled it inside, dropped everything else in, too, and closed the doors. He was hurrying now, leaving.

I heard the elevator chime and the small sliding sound as it started down. With him in it, I hoped, and I lay still under the bed, making myself count to a hundred before I poked my head out. Oh, man! That had been hairy all the way.

I sat on the edge of the bed and flexed my leg. My heart was still bouncing. OK, Andy, take it easy. You're safe now. At least till tomorrow. Nobody will be back till then. No night on the street to worry about. Take it easy.

I was facing one of those long velvet chairs that has a curved back and bendy legs. That's where I'd sleep tonight, not on the clam bed. And I'd be safe from all the dangers of the streets.

There was a phone on the little table beside the chair and another by the bed. Tomorrow I'd try calling Dad again. This time maybe I wouldn't have to talk to that stupid Marigold. Of course, it would mean sneaking out to a phone booth because if I used this phone, the hotel operator would know someone was in the Tower Suite. It would be a dead giveaway. Just as long as I didn't get Marigold again when I called Dad.

"What kind of a name is *that?*" my friend Leah had asked. "She sounds like a plant."

"More like poison ivy," I'd said.

I can't stand Marigold and her prissy English accent and the way she'd sighed this morning when the operator gave her my name and asked if they'd accept the call. I'd stood in the phone booth at the end of Huffer Street, the morning sun warm on my back.

"It's Dad's son," Marigold had yelled. "From America. He's looking for Dad again. He's calling collect."

I'd wanted to punch her out, long distance. My dad wasn't her dad. He'd married her mother, that was all. Who gave her permission to call him "Dad"?

I didn't call Paul Paws "Dad." Where did she get off?

Then Jean came on. Jean is Marigold's mother. I've never met either of them. "We'll accept the call," she said and then she said, "Hello, Andy. Drew's off on a dig." My dad's name's Andrew, same as mine.

"Is he still on the Sutton Hoo burial?" I asked, not because I needed to know but because I wanted her to know that Dad and I kept in touch, that I was important to him. Probably I couldn't fool Jean, though. We both know Dad's been on that dig off and on for about eight years. Jean also probably knows how much he keeps in touch with me. I swallowed.

"Have they found anything new at the site?" I asked.

"Not really. But we're not expecting him home for a while."

I was going to say, "But doesn't he come and go all the time? After all, he's not that far away." I'd looked up the Thames Valley on a map, and I knew that much about it. But I didn't say anything. Instead I tried to picture home for Dad with Jean and Marigold the Plant on Adpar Street, London W2. Home used to be with Mom and me. But that was getting to be a long time ago.

"I'll call him again in a while then," I'd said to Jean. "Cheerio." "Cheerio" is what Dad says instead of "good-bye."

Tomorrow wasn't exactly "in a while." It was sooner than that. Jean probably wouldn't like another collect call. But I'd try anyway. And, with luck, Dad would be there himself. Till then I'd stay where I was.

I had a hard time going to sleep that night because I was jumpy and frightened, after Fred. Also because I was so hungry my stomach hurt. It gurgled and whined, and I thought about how Mamie was going to change the fruit the next morning anyway, so maybe I could take just one little piece.

I did, in the end, getting an apple from the very bottom, putting everything carefully back in place, draping the grapes again.

I ate core and all, partly because I was so hungry and partly to hide the evidence.

I had to use the toilet and that worried me a lot. Should I flush? Someone might hear the sound. But I had to take the chance, and it turned out to be fine because that flush was no louder than a sigh. The other big surprise was that the toilet seat was heated. I'd never known there was such a thing as a heated toilet seat, but, actually, it's a luxury I wouldn't mind having if I were as rich as that bank president.

I tried again to sleep.

The bedroom clock was weird. It beamed the numbers onto the ceiling, a red so pale it was almost pink.

The numbers would have been right way up for some-one lying on the bed. But from the long velvet chair they were all skewed.

I watched them change and change and change, and I told myself again that I wasn't hungry anymore and that I was safe till morning. That this was the perfect hideout.

I guess I slept.

But I wasn't safe.

Because sometime in the night I wakened to a small, muffled noise, to knowing somebody was in the room with me, somebody who hadn't switched on the lights but who had a flashlight with a narrow white beam that was sweeping around. Sweeping in my direction.

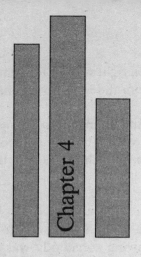

Chapter 4

The flashlight paused for a second, lingering on the glass doors to the balcony. I watched the glare on the windows and felt as frozen as a rabbit caught in the headlights of a car. But then someone stumbled and someone else said, "Sh," and I was unfrozen, knowing that there were two people in the room and that I was really in danger. I had to do something fast.

Soundlessly I slithered off the long chair, crouching low behind it. Anyone shining a light over here would see me. My feet and legs would be right there in plain sight under the chair. I'd taken off my tennies so I wouldn't mark up the pink velvet, and my white socks seemed impossible to miss, like two great blobs of luminous paint. On the ceiling the clock figures said 12:10.

Were these night security guards on their rounds, checking all the rooms that weren't occupied? Would they do that? Wouldn't guards switch on the lights? Or at least have bigger flashlights? Burglars then? They were moving quietly enough.

"This way," one of them whispered, and the other whispered back, "You're sure about this, Fred?" The second voice was a girl's, scared but with a giggle in it, too.

Fred! There couldn't be two Freds in my life in one day. This had to be the same one. He said, "Give me your hand. Just trust old Fred."

The flashlight beam was nowhere close to me, now. I raised my head, peered across the long slope of the chair, and saw two figures against the paleness that gleamed through the windows.

The taller one was carrying a bag. His other hand directed the flashlight toward the feet of the woman.

She was wearing high-heeled shoes with no backs and black stockings with silvery squiggles. This for sure was not Mamie. She and Fred had not come back to take care of the poodle pee.

"Oops," the woman said, and this time she did giggle. Their outstretched hands met, and Fred guided her to the balcony. The curved glass doors slid open.

"So, what do you think?" he asked, and though his voice was low I could hear perfectly.

"Oh, Fred! It's terrific!"

"Was I right or what?"

They stepped outside.

I knew instantly what had happened. Fred hadn't given Mamie back the key. Instead he was taking his girl, or some girl, for a date in the Tower Suite. While they were out there on the balcony, I'd better get myself out of here. I began to crawl. If I could just make it to the door.

Oh, no. They were coming back in. I scrambled for the shell bed and slid under.

"OK, baby, let's see what we've got," Fred said.

They were standing now in front of the dresser. Things clinked. Things rustled.

"This, sweetheart, is champagne," Fred said. "And these glasses are not plastic." There was a *ping* that sounded like a finger being flicked against a glass rim. "Genuine lead crystal—I took them from the kitchen."

"Oh, Fred!"

"Wait till you see the rest. In this container we have a cold chicken salad."

"You *made* it?" Baby squeaked.

"No. Mazzaronni's Deli made it, and it better be good. It cost bucks. In here we have bread sticks. These are cheese slices."

My stomach gurgled, and I squeezed it hard, flattening myself against the carpet. Chicken salad. Bread sticks. I'd even settle for cheese slices, though Mom says they're yellow plastic and not cheese at all, and she never buys them.

32

"And now for the crowning glory! Ta DA!" Fred said with a great flourish.

Baby gasped.

I was almost tempted to poke my head out to see, but I didn't have to because Fred told me.

"Chocolate mousse cake! Hard to carry, but still."

Chocolate mousse cake! There'd be dark crust like an Oreo cookie and a smooth and creamy top. A drip of spit dribbled from my mouth and onto the rug. I wiped it up with my sleeve. Gross!

"I've got paper plates, napkins, little forks."

Baby kept giving moans of admiration.

"I wanted to bring candles," Fred said. "But candles on the balcony might be seen."

"There's a moon anyway," Baby said. "We don't need silly candles. Oh, Freddy! I can't believe it! A midnight picnic at the top of the world."

Their feet were turned toward each other now, and Fred brought the flashlight beam in a slow upward curve. I could only follow the light as far as Baby's shimmery knees.

"You look like a million bucks in that dress," he said, all sincere, and I wanted to jump out and bop him one. He was just like Paul Paws talking to my mom, saying, "I love your hair like that" or "You look wonderful in blue."

I hate those smooth guys who are always turning on the fake charm. And the worst part of it is the way people believe them. Baby! My mom!

Baby was standing on tiptoe now, and I guessed

the two of them were smooching. She bent one leg back and went "Mmmm," the way you do when something's specially delicious. And they hadn't even touched the chocolate mousse cake yet.

And then I saw my tennies. I'd taken them off so I wouldn't dirty up the pink chair. There they were, placed neatly side by side. Fred and Baby couldn't miss them.

"Shall we dine?" Fred asked, and Baby said, "Oh, let's. I'll carry the champagne."

I peered out from under the bedspread, hardly daring to breathe. He had the flashlight directed at the glass doors of the shadowy balcony. Its beam shimmered back on their two figures. Maybe he would miss the shoes after all. Maybe he'd be so anxious to . . .

He stopped. The light hit my Reeboks, circled them, zoomed back to pick up on them again.

"What's this?" Fred's voice was a whisper. He bent and lifted one by its Superman laces.

I pulled back under the bed as far as I could go. Oh, no! Oh, help!

"These weren't here today," he said. "I'd have seen them for sure."

Baby gave a nervous squeak. "Fred . . . the suite's occupied!"

"Naw. I checked. But somebody's been here since I left. Some kid."

My heart was choking me, its beat loud as a bongo drum.

"Wait here," Fred said. "I'm sure the place is empty, but I'm going to look around and make sure."

"I'm not waiting by myself," Baby said. "I'm coming with you."

I watched their feet leave. Did he have my shoe with him, or had he put it on the pink chair or on the dresser? He hadn't put it back by the other one. He and Baby were going all around the suite. Small drifts of whispered words came back to me.

"Nobody here."

"No luggage."

"I told you. I checked the register."

They were back in the bedroom.

"It's just the way I left it earlier. The fruit bowl, the newspapers. And look." I heard the closet doors slide open. "Here's my stuff that I left for tomorrow."

"But whose shoes could they be, Fred?"

"How do I know? Maybe one of the managers came up here for something and brought his kid. It has to be a kid. Who else would have laces with Superman on them?"

"Maybe Mamie?" Baby began. "She has a couple of boys. Doesn't she always do the Tower . . ."

Fred interrupted. "Not Mamie. I haven't given her back her key yet. How do you think we got in here?"

"You should turn the shoes in, Fred, and tell them downstairs. I'm sure the managers aren't supposed to come up here and bring their kids and just use . . ."

Fred sounded annoyed. "How can I turn them

in? What would I say I was doing back up here? Get *real*, will you?"

"You'd better turn them in tomorrow then. We can't leave old beat-up shoes like that in the Tower Suite." Baby's voice brightened. "I know, we could set them outside the door."

"For the shoeshine fairy?" Fred asked, mean and cranky.

"But what if someone comes back looking for them tonight when we're here? Uh uh. We'd lose our jobs. I'm not risking that, Freddy. Let's get out of here."

Go, I thought. Go. But leave my shoes. I can't do anything without my shoes.

"I know." Baby gave a little excited hop. "We could go across to Peppertree Park and eat there at one of the tables, in the moonlight. That would be almost as romantic, Fred."

"Sure. And we could invite the winos and the crack dealers. They'd love it, too."

"Well, you do what you like. I'm leaving."

"I guess we could just eat in my van." Fred gave his bad-tempered grunt. "Brother! Eight dollars and ninety-eight cents for that chicken salad. I might as well have bought bologna sandwiches."

He set my shoe down next to the other one. "There's something weird about this," he said. "It doesn't make sense."

I heard some clickings and rustlings, and I guessed

Baby was packing away the food. "Let's go," she whispered. "Forget about the shoes."

"We're going. We're going. Just take it easy."

The small circle of light bobbed toward the door, followed by the two pairs of feet; then the yellow light bounced back, hopping around until it found the shoes.

From where I lay it was as if the Reeboks were caught in a spotlight, like part of a TV commercial. It hung on them for a long time before Fred clicked the flashlight off.

I waited and waited before I came out. Shivers ran up my legs as I tiptoed past the shoes and over to the window. No need to tiptoe. I was in my socks and on a rug and there was no one here. But I tiptoed anyway.

I tiptoed into the living room and swung the telescope so that it pointed straight down, sliding it around in search of Fred and Baby coming out of the hotel. I guessed they wouldn't use the front entrance so I slid the scope back and forth between the doors from the smaller lobbies. There weren't too many people around. Two men stood talking on the flagstones at the front. The lens was so strong I could see the double chins on one of them shake as he laughed. A guy and a girl hailed a taxi, and the doorman ran to open the cab door for them. The brass buttons on his gray uniform shone in the lamplight.

Two other people were crossing the street now.

Fred and Baby! The silver spiders squiggled on her stockings, her high heels wobbled. Fred carried the bag, and she clung to the crook of his arm. Dark, empty cars lined a side street. That's where they were headed. They stopped, and I saw the square bulk of a van.

Fred set the bag down and opened the door for her. What manners!

I twisted the focus and got it clearer, saw that the van was blue and that there were zigzag letters on the side, Surf Rider. The wavy white lines on the roof were meant to be the ocean.

Fred had disappeared around the driver's side. I waited for the headlights to go on and for them to take off, but all was dark and quiet. I wondered if they were picnicking, eating the eight dollars and ninety-eight cents chicken salad and that mousse cake. Were they in the front or in the back? Did Fred have a little table there? If they were using candles or inside van lights there was no glimmer of them.

I sat by the window, watching till my eyes ached. Now and then I think I dropped off to sleep, my head against the smooth black arm of the telescope, because there were gaps in the time.

And then, when I looked again, the van had gone.

They wouldn't come back, would they? No. It was ten minutes past two.

I tiptoed back to the bedroom and squirmed under the bed. So tired. So sleepy. No way to stay awake any longer.

But I lifted the bedspread an inch from the floor to look at my shoes where Fred had left them. I wanted to hide them underneath here with me. But what if he *did* come back and found them missing? Then he'd really search the place, in the closets, under the bed. Better to leave them there till morning. When he came to clean the rug, the shoes would be gone, and he'd figure someone had come in even earlier than he had and taken them. That's what I hoped he'd figure.

"Forget about the shoes," Baby had advised him.

Why did I have this horrible feeling that he wasn't going to?

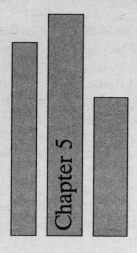

Chapter 5

It was six-thirty in the morning.

A long time after Fred and Baby had left, I'd crawled out again from under the bed and figured out how to set the alarm on the ceiling clock. I'd have to be out of here in the morning, early and fast.

I got my shoes and put them on, took the stairs down two floors and picked up the elevator from there. That seemed the safest way. Suppose someone was waiting on the thirty-fourth and I came sailing from above like some sort of angel? Better to be careful. But the only one waiting at the elevator was a sea gull, perched on the rail outside. He arched his neck and stared angrily at me as the elevator moved and he had to take off, dropping beside me, then sailing away.

I looked down at my feet, and I wished I could

get a change of shoes, or at least a change of laces, because Fred was going to remember these. Superman laces! The only reason I wore them every day, anyway, was because Dad had sent them.

"For you, sport," he'd said on the scribbled note. "I know you're fond of the caped avenger."

"Isn't that just like him?" Mom had said to Paul Paws. "He's five years behind the times. Shows how much he knows about his son. Andy hasn't as much as mentioned Superman since he was six years old."

"What do you mean?" I'd argued. "I *love* Superman." I'd pulled out my old laces and threaded these in. They were the stupidest looking things, to tell the truth. Leah had pointed at them and screwed up her face. "Are those a joke?"

"No," I'd said, not wanting to explain that I was stuck with them, or why.

Brother, I wished old Fred hadn't seen them. I wondered if there was anywhere around the Countess International where you could buy ordinary laces. Probably not. They probably didn't sell necessities within ten blocks of here.

Early as it was, there were a few guests walking briskly through the lobby and two clerks on duty behind the desk. But in these smaller lobbies there was no long counter and no assistant manager to look at me suspiciously and shout out questions.

I kept wondering if one of the clerks had talked to Fred and was noticing my shoes.

"The darnedest thing last night," Fred would have said. "I sneaked Baby up to the Tower Suite and somebody had left . . ."

I walked fast and pushed open the curved doors.

Cool off, Andy. Half the world wears Reeboks. I saw on TV they even wear them in Africa with their loincloths and things. But do they have Superman laces?

It was cold outside, and I pulled my hands up inside the sleeves of my sweatshirt. Somewhere, not too far away, church bells were ringing, and I remembered that it was Sunday morning, which was why there wasn't too much traffic.

I took a deep breath of the gray, damp San Francisco morning, and all at once I felt good. I was still here, wasn't I? A whole night had passed, and I was still in one piece. Mom would be crazy with worry by now. And, by tomorrow morning, she'd be crazier still! "I wish I hadn't said that to him yesterday, Paul, but it was the truth."

He'd stroke her hair and agree with her. He always agrees with her. And he always strokes her hair.

"It's time I told you the way it really is, Andy," she'd said to me. "I'm tired of being the heavy around here."

She called that the *truth*.

She'd be sorry now all right.

I felt so good, I gave a little skip and a hop. OK! Things were working out fine.

"Andy?"

Behind me someone was calling my name.

Mom?

My heart began skipping and hopping, too, it was so filled with joy and relief. She was sorry. She'd seen how much she'd hurt me, and she'd been out all night looking, hoping she'd find—I swung around.

"Andy! I thought that was you!" It was the woman who'd been in the elevator with me yesterday. Mrs. Saint. She and her husband came hurrying toward me. Not Mom after all.

I couldn't believe how awful I felt. What had made me think it would be her, anyway?

"Couldn't miss that Forty Niners sweatshirt," Mr. Saint said. He was wearing a tweed coat that came to just below his knees and a squashed tweed hat with a feather in it, and she had on a bright red coat with a humungous scarf over one shoulder and a little black bowler hat, the kind Laurel and Hardy wear in their old movies. I think on her it was probably OK.

"You're out and about early," she said.

"I guess so," I said.

"Taking a walk like us, are you?" the man asked and I nodded.

Mrs. Saint frowned a little. "I suppose it's safe enough for you to be out here wandering around by yourself? As long as you stay close to the hotel, anyway. Your mother thinks it's all right?"

"Oh, she's still asleep," I said, which was probably true since this was a Sunday morning. Of course, it wasn't supposed to be a normal Sunday morning for her, since her son had just run away, but still.

"We're just on our way back to the hotel. We've had quite a walk, all the way to Fisherman's Wharf and back."

"And we've worked up quite an appetite," Mr. Saint added and winked.

Mrs. Saint cocked her head. I expected her hat to slide off, but it didn't. "I don't suppose you could join us for breakfast? We'd love to have you. Unless you think your mother would object?"

"Do you like sausages and hotcakes?" Mr. Saint asked me. "They have great sausages and hotcakes in that hotel restaurant . . . what's it called, honey? Madelena's?"

My mouth watered so suddenly that I had to swallow hard. "It'll be all right with my mom. She doesn't eat much for breakfast, anyway. Usually just juice and toast. She always has it in bed on Sunday mornings."

I had a quick flash of Paul Paws fixing her tray, putting a rose from the garden on it, whistling as he carried it up to her, his short brown robe showing his hairy legs. I saw me sitting by myself at the kitchen table, listening to them laughing upstairs.

"Mom doesn't care what *I* eat," I said.

Mrs. Saint played with the fringe of her scarf. "I'll

tell you what," she said. "Why don't we go inside and you just scoot up to your room and check with your mom? Tell her we're in room 3009, and she can check on us at the desk if she'd like. And if she has no objections, you come on down and join us in Madelena's."

"Or you could use the house phone," Mr. Saint suggested, and then he said to his wife, "Why don't *you* speak to his mother yourself?"

"That's OK," I said quickly. "That'd wake her up. It will be better if I just run up and leave a note."

We were crossing the main lobby now, me walking between the two of them, Mr. Assistant Manager beaming at us from behind his shining counter. See, I thought, wanting to stick my tongue out at him. See how respectable I am? He probably thought they were my grandma and grandpa. I wished they were. They left me at the restaurant door.

"If you don't come back we won't worry. We'll figure your mother has other plans," Mrs. Saint said. She was so nice. I really liked her a lot.

I rode up to the twenty-ninth floor and straight down again, and then I thought I hadn't let enough time go by so I rode up and down again. A gray-haired lady in a jogging suit was standing by the elevators, probably waiting for someone, and she smiled at me. "It's fun, isn't it?" she asked. "Last time we brought my grandsons to stay in this hotel they rode that elevator up and down all day long."

I smiled back. She seemed nice, too. Maybe this was my lucky day.

"All right?" Mrs. Saint asked when the hostess led me to their table. There were three places set and three glasses of orange juice. "We had high hopes, you see," she said.

A waiter in a white jacket with a napkin across his arm came gliding over, all smiles. "I think we can go ahead and order the rest now," Mr. Saint told him.

I tucked my feet with the giveaway laces under the chair. Madelena's didn't seem like Fred's kind of place, but you never could tell. He might even work part-time as a waiter. I ate a great breakfast anyway. I had pancakes and four sausages and three bran muffins dripping butter and filled with fat California raisins. The waiter said they were from California, and he probably knew. He'd winked at me. "They're the kind that dance. Careful they don't dance off your plate."

"My," Mrs. Saint said. "I'd forgotten boys can eat that much. We have five grandchildren, three of them boys, but we can't see them very often. They all live far away."

I found a raisin that had danced away and popped it into my mouth. At the table next to us, two men were talking in a foreign language.

"Russian," Mr. Saint whispered.

I glanced across at them. "My friend Leah talks

to a guy in Russia all the time. Leah's a ham radio operator. Once she talked to somebody in Japan."

"Your friend knows all those languages?" Mr. Saint raised his eyebrows.

"They don't understand each other," I explained. "They just talk." The Saints laughed as though I'd made a tremendous joke.

Mr. Saint ordered me hot chocolate to finish off.

I was feeling really great now . . . warm, funny, and full. I was also feeling smelly, since I'd been wearing the same clothes for two days. I hoped the Saints didn't notice. We waited for the hot chocolate to arrive.

"So?" Mrs. Saint had taken off her coat and scarf but she still wore the hat with her red dress. "Are your parents both staying here?"

Uh-oh. Trouble.

I shook my head. "My dad's in England."

"In England? That's nice. Is he on business?"

"Sort of. He's an archaeologist. He's on a dig, the Sutton Hoo burial dig. Have you heard of it? It's pretty important. They're excavating an old boat. He lives in London," I added. "He and my mom are divorced." I don't even know why I said that. It must have been that the Saints looked so interested. Fortunately, the hot chocolate arrived then, and I hoped the subject was closed.

"Do you get to visit him now and then?" Mr. Saint asked.

"I'm going to, pretty soon." I bent my head and took a sip and looked up just in time to see the Saints exchanging knowing, sympathetic glances. "It's OK," I told them. "He wants me."

"I'm sure he does," Mrs. Saint said in the softest, nicest voice. "Divorce can be very hard on fathers."

I nodded. "Sometimes I call him, collect." I watched the Russians at the next table, who seemed to be arguing over the bill.

One time I'd heard Paul Paws say to Mom, "Why doesn't the creep ever call the kid? For heaven's sake, it's his *birthday*."

"Oh, well," Mom said.

Where did Paul Paws get off calling my dad a creep? And why couldn't Mom just tell him to shut up? I could have told them why Dad didn't call. He didn't want to get Paul Paws by mistake, that was why. Or even Mom, probably.

"One of our sons got divorced," Mrs. Saint was saying, "and then his wife remarried out of state, and her husband wasn't that nice to our two grandchildren."

I nodded. "My stepfather is not nice to me at all."

I looked from one of them to the other and felt my face getting red because that wasn't true. Paul Paws was OK with me. If he'd been Leah's father, I'd probably think he was an all right guy. Once he'd even taken me on a night hike up Mount Tamalpais so we could look at the stars. Paul Paws is very big on stars. He'd bought me a star map and brought it along on the hike to show me how to find Polaris and the Big Dipper. It's just that I don't like the way he is with my mom.

"He doesn't *hurt* you, does he?" Mr. Saint's voice bristled, and his face had gone red, too.

"No," I said. "Uh uh." I took a big drink of my hot chocolate. "Well, thanks a whole lot for the breakfast. It was great. I gotta go."

Mr. Saint was looking at me seriously. He took a wallet from his jacket pocket and gave me a business card. On it was printed Ackerman Industries, with an address in New Orleans and a phone number. In the bottom right corner it said Doug Ackerman, President.

He stubbed at the number with his thumb. "You call us if you're in trouble. Call collect, the way you do to your dad. We're used to it from our grandkids."

"Thanks." I put the card carefully in my jeans pocket, the pocket that didn't have the stolen money.

Mr. Saint, who was really Mr. Ackerman, I guess, helped Mrs. Saint-Ackerman on with her coat and scarf. She gave her little round hat a tap and said, "Right!"

We all shook hands.

"Don't worry," I told them. "I'm going to call my dad this morning. We're going to arrange for my visit."

"Great. Good luck, Andy. We probably won't see you again."

"Come down to New Orleans and watch some

good football," Mr. Saint-Ackerman called after me. They waited by the restaurant door, and I felt them watching me as I crossed the main lobby to go outside.

The clocks above the desk told me it was five minutes to eight in San Francisco, five minutes to four in London.

Sunday afternoon . . . teatime, Dad called it. He'd probably be home by now.

Murphy, the doorman who'd been watching us, opened the doors for me with a flourish. I wondered if he got a tip every time he did that. Well, not from me.

I imagined the Saints heading toward the elevator asking each other, "Why doesn't the boy just use the room telephone?" and Mr. Saint saying in that gruff voice, "Probably doesn't want to talk to his dad in front of that stepfather. Too bad."

I had to walk a couple of blocks before I found a phone. It was the kind that hangs on a wall on the way into a gas station. I was beginning to get nervous about calling collect again and so soon. Except that this was an emergency. I had to get Dad, and I couldn't use up my cash just in case. He'd understand. I put in my money and told the operator the number, my name, and that this was a collect call. I pocketed the refund after it came rattling back to me.

Someone had written on the wall above the phone, I'm Waiting in the Wings. What did that mean? How could you wait in wings? Maybe it started out to be swings and the *s* got blotted out.

The phone was ringing in faraway London now. It didn't even sound like an American phone. I was hoping and hoping that Dad would answer.

"Hi, Andy," he'd say. Or "Hi, son." I hoped it wouldn't be prissy Marigold again.

It was Jean. "Hello. Jean Dubin here."

"I have a collect call from California from Mr. Andy Dubin," the operator said. "Will you accept the charges?"

Quick as anything I said, "It's an emergency, Jean," so she'd know.

There was total silence from the London end.

"Hello," the operator said. I could hear her talking to somebody else on the side, probably one of her operator friends, saying something about "It's across the street from Macy's." Then she said in her business voice, "Ma'am? Will you accept . . ."

"Andy," Jean said. "You really mustn't keep calling all the time. He calls all the time, operator," she added.

"Wait," I said. "Wait, operator. I can pay for the call. Wait."

I was pulling money out of my pocket. A five-dollar bill, one of Paul Paws's, drifted down and began to blow away. I let the phone dangle and grabbed for it. Why hadn't I brought some quarters and dimes?

"How much is it?" I asked. "I've got . . ."

"Your father's still not here, Andy," Jean said. "I don't know when he'll be back. Not for three weeks or so. He never tells me for sure." I thought she sounded sad, but it was probably just because of the long distance.

Then the operator butted in, mad at both of us. "If you want to place this call, please . . ."

I could still hear her talking in her distant, tinny voice as I hung up the phone.

I'm waiting in the wings, I thought. I'm waiting in the swings. My father wasn't there, and three weeks was forever. How was I going to hang on that long?

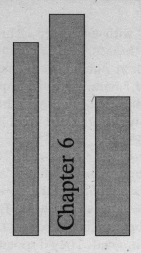

Chapter 6

I began walking. An empty cable car rattled past me on its way up Powell. Later in the day it would be jammed with tourists.

I don't think I meant to go there, but pretty soon I discovered I was headed for home. Or at least in that direction.

Mamie had said she always went up to the Tower Suite early, so I'd stay away for a while and give her and Fred time to finish. Awful if I went back too soon, and they were both there, and Fred would take one look at my feet and say, "Aha! The mysterious shoes with the Superman laces!"

I decided I might as well walk in this direction as in any other.

The sun was breaking through the morning dampness, warm on my shoulders, and my mind beat out a little tune that kept time with each step. Three weeks, three. Three weeks, three.

I'd just take a quick look at our house to see if everything was OK. I hoped I hadn't given Mom a bad headache. Sometimes she gets one when she's worried. Not that I'd show myself to her or anything like that. I'd just check things out.

Three weeks, three. Three weeks, three. The words bounced in my head, and I couldn't figure out how to get rid of them. How could I hide in the Tower Suite for that long? Three days was one thing. But three weeks? I couldn't keep walking through the lobbies hoping I wouldn't be noticed. They'd spot me for sure.

Was I at Worth Street already? I must have been walking fast, beating out my three-step time. Tom's health food store on our corner was open. Tom knows me. But did he know I'd left home? I stood for a minute, trying to decide if it was too risky to go in. Maybe. But then I went in anyway and ordered a banana shake to go. Banana shakes are Mom's favorite. I asked them to put a lid on it, and I carried it carefully, two-handed, and all the time I was walking I wasn't sure what I meant to do. Was I going to give this to her or what?

There aren't too many streets like ours left in San Francisco, and most ordinary people, like us, can't afford homes in the city. But this house used to be my grandma's and my mom slept in my room when she was a little girl. The pink azalea bush outside the window was small then. Now it's gigantic.

Everything was Sunday quiet on the street. The *Chronicle* still lay fat and bundled in most of the driveways, and there was our house, small and old, squished between the Nolans on one side and the Manriquezes on the other. Nicer than theirs, though, because our grass is always bright green and there are hanging baskets on our porch that Paul Paws keeps filled with flowers. Our little lemon tree had two green lemons on it. The day Paul Paws planted it, Mom had gone out to watch. She'd bent over and rubbed the top of his head and said "Hi, sweetheart" in that teasing, loving way she has when she speaks to him. Actually, she seems to like touching him as much as he likes pawing her.

Her Honda was in the driveway with Paul Paws's green pickup behind it.

I stopped to lick a spill that had trickled down the side of the cup before I stepped around the truck.

Through the screen door I could see Paul Paws in the kitchen, standing barefoot at the stove, his back to me. He was wearing his brown robe.

I took a step closer. The yellow tray was on the table, all set up with Mom's flowered cup and saucer and his green mug. I saw the rose from the garden, the dappled honey jar with the bee on top that I'd bought for her in Monterey. The rich, morning smell of coffee drifted to me.

"Hang on, sweetheart," Paul Paws called. "Brunch is on the way."

I watched him start up the stairs, carrying the tray, and I thought, Sunday morning and everything the same. Andy's gone, but who cares.

I set the banana shake on the top step and walked backward down the path.

The Nolans' dog, Skeeter, wasn't around. He was either inside or he'd jumped the fence again. Skeeter's a good jumper. I was sorry he wasn't here. I sure would have liked to see him. I walked faster and faster. Just let me out of here.

There was Leah's apartment building, her window on the top floor, the big ham radio aerial tall and shining on the roof. Since I couldn't see Skeeter, I sure wished I could see Leah, but there was no way.

I was feeling pretty sorry for myself, and I said out loud, "Quit it. You have a great hideout. Three weeks there isn't too terrible. You'll just be careful, that's all."

I stopped to wipe my eyes on my sleeve and stare way up at Leah's windows. Could I throw a rock that far? Hey! Why didn't I just call and invite her to come visit me? She'd flip when she saw my place. I imagined the look on her face when she saw the sunken bath, the telescope, and the TV behind the carved Chinese doors, and I felt cheered already.

I called from outside the Seven-Eleven, using the money the operator had returned to me when I couldn't get Dad.

Of course, it was Leah's little brother, Parker, who answered. It's always Parker who answers.

I tried to disguise my voice. "Leah, please."

"Andy? Is that you?"

"Sh," I said. "Keep it down. I don't want your mom to hear. And don't tell anyone, Parker, or you'll be in big trouble. I mean it. Go get Leah."

"She's talking to Pud."

I groaned. I hate it when Leah talks to Pud, her ham radio friend in St. Paul, Minnesota. Actually, I hate Pud. Pud's father has a cabin on Coon Lake and they go up there in winter to ice fish. Once Pud caught a twelve-pounder.

"It must have been a pretty big ice hole if he could drag a twelve-pounder through it," I'd told Leah, but she'd just shrugged. Leah believes everything Pud tells her. They talk for hours. If I didn't know I was Leah's best friend, I'd think maybe Pud was.

"Tell Leah I'm on the phone," I told Parker. "Whisper. Tell her to leave Pud and come."

"I'll tell her it's *another* one of her boyfriends." Parker sniggered.

"Try not to be such a dweeb, Parker," I told him.

I was glad that she came right away. I hoped she was so happy to hear from me that she'd left Victor Pudinski in mid brag.

"Andy?" she whispered. "Where are you? How are you doing?"

For once I felt more thrilling than Pud.

"I'm doing fine," I told her, cocky as could be. "You should see the hideout I found."

"Where? Is it safe? Is it somewhere close?"

"I don't know about safe. I almost got caught last night. I had to take cover. Man, it was hairy!" I was beginning to be almost glad about last night. What a story!

"But couldn't you just come home, Andy? Your mom . . ."

Then I heard her say, "It's a friend from school, Dad. I'll be through in a second." She sighed. "My dad needs the phone," she told me. "We've got to be fast."

"OK. Can you meet me at two? I want to show you my hideout. It's kudos, no kidding. Can you make some excuse?"

"I guess so."

"OK. You know the park across from the Countess International? Meet me there." I was feeling better all the time. The thing to do was look on this as an adventure. I'd figure something out about the three weeks.

"Could you bring me some underwear and a sweatshirt, Leah? And some food? Does your mom have an extra jar of peanut butter and maybe some cheese?"

58

"Hey!" Leah sounded alarmed.

"OK, forget the food. I'm full anyway. Bring the clothes and listen . . . this is the most important. Could you bring me shoelaces?"

"Huh?"

"No, I mean it. I'm desperate to have shoelaces. Ordinary ones. Oh, and could you bring a towel?" If I had a towel, I could shower, and Mamie wouldn't know.

There was silence and then Leah said, "This sounds peculiar to me."

"Never mind," I said. "Just do it. See you at two."

"Wait," Leah said. "I have to tell you something. Pud's mother just had identical twins. One's a boy and one's a girl. Pud's calling them Pea and Pod."

"Pea, Pod, and Pud," I said. "Cute."

"Yeah, isn't it." Leah never seems to know when I'm being sarcastic.

"But how can they be identical if one's a boy and one's a girl?" I asked.

"I dunno. Pud says his mom put nail polish on one twin's toe. It's the only way she knows the difference."

"That's amazing," I said. "If one's a boy and one's a girl. See you at two," I added and hung up fast before I had to listen to any more Pud stories. That guy is so full of it.

I took one backward glance at Worth Street. From here all I could see of our house was the corner of

59

the roof. I wondered if Mom had found the banana shake yet, and suddenly I realized how dumb I'd been to leave it. She'd know it was me. We buy each other banana shakes on special occasions. Or to say we're sorry if we've had one of our fights. "Andy's been here," she'd say. "I knew he wouldn't go far."

Would she say it in that soft, loving way or would she be laughing at me, sharing the joke with Paul Paws? My heart was beating awfully fast.

Could I get the cup back? Would it still be there?

I went quickly along the street again, keeping my head down, hoping I wouldn't be seen. I hadn't worried about that earlier.

"And why not, Andy?" I asked myself and I knew why not. I'd *wanted* her to see me. I'd wanted her to say, "I'm so glad you're home. Don't ever, ever leave us again."

I didn't meet anyone I knew. Some guy was washing his car, rock music heating the air around him. Two cats slept in the pale sun on the Nolans' roof.

I got behind Paul Paws's truck. The paper cup was exactly where I'd left it. Upstairs, the window of Mom's bedroom was open but I didn't hear any voices. The two of them were probably in bed, drinking coffee and happily reading the paper, the way they always do Sunday mornings.

Carefully I tiptoed to the step and lifted the cup. A column of ants paraded up the drip on the side and circled the rim under the lid. I held the cup away from me as I walked. The Balatonis never bring their garbage cans in from the curb after pickup day, something that drives Mom crazy. They were there, lidless, in their usual place. I dumped the cup in, and I knew that I wasn't dumping only the banana shake.

"Andy's been and gone," I said, and then I hurried back along Worth Street. This time I didn't cry. And I didn't look back.

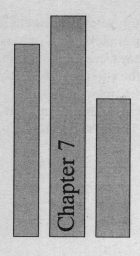

Chapter 7

I was careful going up the elevator and careful stepping out, too, standing by the suite doors listening till my ears hurt. There was no sound.

Fresh flowers filled the vase on the marble table, reflecting in the mirror. Mamie had been here all right, and so had Fred. I saw the damp spots on the rug and the bottom of the drape. His big vacuum and the cleaning materials were gone from the closet. So everything was clear and safe for my visitor.

The clock figures on the ceiling said 1:05. About an hour to wait. What if she didn't come? She would, though. Leah always does what she says she'll do. I prowled around, planning what I would show her, how I'd act out Fred and Baby last night. Thinking about Fred made me nervous again, and I went back to the elevator. If only there was some way to block it off. But if there was, I didn't know it. Anyway, Fred wouldn't have a key now. I was safe.

1:15. Today's papers were neatly stacked on the table. I took the *Chronicle* apart, separated the comics and the classified section that had the personals in it. Twice before I'd found people offering cheap plane tickets to London. Once someone wanted to swap one for two Super Bowl seats. That was the year the Niners beat the Bengals. There were no airline tickets today, but someone was giving a three-hundred-dollar reward for a ginger cat that answered to the name Barnstable. Three hundred dollars! Once TWA had a special one-way flight to London for less than that. Maybe I should go look for that cat! Naw. What chance would I have of finding it? Zilch. I put the paper neatly back together and slid it in with the others.

1:50. It was early to go to the park but I didn't want to sit here and think about how far away London is, about Mom and Paul Paws and the two of them not even missing me. About those long three weeks.

A tour group was coming in, and the lobby downstairs overflowed with suitcases and people and kids wearing very short shorts and kneesocks. I slipped through the crowd and jaywalked across the street.

Boys were playing baseball on the scratchy grass. Two dogs galloped around, yelping with joy, and white clouds raced across the sky. The park was nice during the day. It was just at night that it changed, like Jekyll and Hyde.

I sat on the pedestal of the St. Francis statue with St. Francis himself towering over me and stroked the head of one of the stone birds he was feeding. I think they were pigeons. The concrete under his foot had broken away. I poked out the dead leaves and dirt. One of the dogs ran over to sniff at my tennis shoe. It probably did smell pretty good, to a dog.

I was thinking I should just have pulled out these dumb laces and gone without, when I spotted Leah turning the corner. She had on her red windbreaker; her striped red-and-yellow backpack drooped like a parachute from one shoulder. Too bad I'd forgotten to tell her to dress inconspicuously—too late now.

It was funny watching her. Leah is little. Her hair is blond and kind of skimpy. Sometimes I can see the pinkness of her head underneath, like a rabbit's stomach. I told her that once, but, believe me, I never mentioned it again. Today she had her hair in some sort of ponytail right on the top of her head. I swear, Leah can do the strangest things to herself.

She'd seen me now. "Hi, Andy!"

"Hi." I ran across the grass to meet her. "How did you get away?"

She crouched to scoop up the baseball that was hurtling in her direction and slow curve it back. "Mom and Dad took Parker to see *The Little Mermaid*. I told them not to because it's too scary, but they never listen. I'm supposed to be doing homework. They told me not to open the door to anyone.

I figure it's OK to open it just while I get out and in." She patted the backpack. "I've got everything you asked for."

"The laces, too?"

"Yeah. I stopped at Thrifty. They cost a dollar twenty-nine. You owe me. No hurry though."

"Can you find them for me fast?" I asked.

"Sure."

We sat while I pulled out the Superman laces and threaded the new ones in. There was a green trash can nearby, and I wavered for a couple of seconds, wondering if I should dump Superman the way I'd dumped the banana shake. But I couldn't. Anyway, I'd put them back in my shoes the minute I got on the plane, before I met Dad. Three weeks from now. He'd like it that I was wearing them. I shoved them deep in my pocket, and I thought Fred would never recognize me, not even if we stood toe to toe. It was like wearing a disguise.

Leah tugged at her brush-top ponytail, then picked a daisy that was growing up through the short park grass. "I have to tell you something. The cops are seriously looking for you, Andy. They're starting a house-to-house search, everything. Your mom went to the station and reported you missing this morning."

"I happen to know that she slept in this morning and had breakfast in bed."

"So? It was *late* in the morning." Leah's voice

was as sharp as glass. "Have you been spying on her, or what? I suppose you know what time she got into bed last night, too?"

I shook my head.

"No? It was real late, I can tell you that. . . . Anyway . . ." Leah set the daisy carefully on the park bench. "The police are searching, I'm telling you. If you don't want to be found, you'd better stay out of sight."

"Well, I sure don't want to be found."

I glanced around. The sidewalks were crammed with tourists, and cars moved in a slow, steady stream in both directions. Sunday traffic had picked up. On the side street, in front of the automatic teller at the bank, a cop car was parked, facing away from us.

"Let's go," I said.

"Where?" Leah asked.

"To my hideout." I nodded toward the hotel. "In there."

Leah gasped. "Are you kidding? In the *hotel?*"

The way she said it made me grin.

"I told you you were going to like it."

We went to the crosswalk at the corner farthest from the parked police car. "I wonder why Mom bothered to tell them I was missing," I said.

"Don't be such a dweeb, Andy. You know why." Leah was shading her eyes, looking up at a helicopter buzzing like a giant hornet between city and sky. "I bet that's the police."

66

It was. I knew by the color. "Just because it's there doesn't mean it's looking for me," I said.

"Doesn't mean it isn't, either," Leah said.

"Aw, they're probably just watching the traffic. How could they think they'd spot me? There are too many people. It would be like looking for Barnstable."

"Who?"

"Never mind."

The lights changed, and we hurried across the street. I kept my head lowered, just in case.

"Going through the lobby's tricky," I told Leah. "Stay cool. Act as if you belong here. And don't look straight at anybody in a hotel uniform."

Leah nodded. "I can do that. No problem."

The tour group was still milling around and that helped. I walked confidently toward the elevator, Leah striding beside me. It was nice not to worry about my feet since I had so many other things to worry about. When the last person got off on the twenty-sixth floor, I used the key.

"Where did you get *that?*" Leah asked. "What are you doing?"

"Beaming us up," I said.

To say that Leah was majorly boggled by the Tower Suite would be no exaggeration.

"If you like, you can tell Pud how neat my hideout is," I told her. And I was thinking, Let him try to top *this* with his identical twins.

"I won't. Unless you want the whole world to know where you are. Unless you want someone to call the police. The airways are open."

"Oh," I said. "Right."

But the thought that the police were out looking for me didn't seem real. There were too many full-on criminals around for them to worry about me.

I let Leah look through the telescope and sweep it in a circle to get the view. I let her touch the heated toilet seat.

"Have you tried this?" she asked.

"Of course." Talking about the toilet seat with Leah was embarrassing, so I quickly guided her toward the bathroom mirrors, letting her see how they reflected us about a hundred times in each direction. Andy and Leah, Leah and Andy, getting smaller and smaller till we were miles away and each the size of Tom Thumb. Leah wiggled her fingers over her head and I did, too.

"Just don't touch the glass," I warned. "Fingerprints. Mamie might get suspicious."

"Who's Mamie?" Leah asked as we went back to the bedroom.

I settled myself cross-legged on the rug close to the shell bed and patted the floor beside me. "If anybody comes, dive underneath quick, like this." I showed her, then wriggled back out.

"You mean somebody might?"

"Maybe," I said, very, very cool. "But I think we're safe for now."

"Aren't you scared that the room—I mean the *suite*—might get rented? Then what would you do?"

"It won't."

She sat next to me while I told her about finding the key, about Mamie and Fred and Baby and almost getting caught. "But the police would never think of looking for me up here," I said.

Leah nodded. "True. How long are you going to stay?"

"A few weeks, that's all."

"Wow! You think you can make it that long?"

I shrugged. "Why not? Let me see what you brought."

She had brought everything I'd asked for, plus extras.

"This is my dad's underwear," she said, holding up a large pair of striped boxer shorts. "But he has tons. He'll never miss it. I know they're humungous, but Parker's would be too small for you. The sweat-shirt's mine." It was the color of hot dog mustard and had Special Sneak Preview written on it. "You can have it for keeps," she said. "I never wear it."

No wonder, I thought.

She'd brought a small can of luncheon meat. "The key to open it is there on the side," she said. "Mom got it in a Christmas basket about three years ago. She won't notice I've taken it."

There was a loaf of squishy bread, the kind I hate, a half package of Oreo cookies, a blue towel, and the map of the stars that Paul Paws had bought me. "I borrowed it, remember?" Leah said. "I thought you might want it. I thought you might be outside . . . you know, in your hideout, and you'd like to know where you were."

"I'd know where I was without that," I said. "And anyway, I hate the stars."

Leah gave me a look.

I've noticed before that she doesn't join in when I talk mean about Paul Paws. Once she'd even said I was making it hard for him on purpose. *I* was making it hard for *him!* Is that a joke or what?

"You can have the map," I told her. "Keep it in exchange for the sweatshirt."

"OK. And I brought this."

I looked at what she was holding, and I knew what it was. But I could hardly believe it. Her Easi-Talkie! Her greatest treasure and a big part of her ham radio equipment. Once I'd picked it up in her room and she'd yelled at me to put it down. Now she held it toward me.

"You want me to take it?" I asked. "But . . ."

"All you have to do is flip it on. Slide this bar on the side up when you want to talk and down when you want to listen. Don't touch that knob on the top. I've set it to a channel that's not used much. I'll keep tuned into it all the time. Just call my number WA6WXG. . . . I've written it down for you."

She fished a scrap of paper out of the pocket of

her windbreaker, gave it to me, and pushed the Easi-Talkie into my other hand.

The Easi-Talkie is smaller than a walkie-talkie and has an aerial on top. Leah reached out and periscoped the aerial up and down. "Raise this when you want to use it. The whole thing clips on your belt, see?"

I pulled the aerial, slid the bar up, and read from the paper. "Are you there, WA6WXG?"

I felt a bit dumb.

"I'm not there because I'm here and my Yaesu's not turned on." Her Yaesu's the big box, like an old-fashioned radio with knobs and buttons, that sits on her desk. That's where she stays for hours, fiddling with the knobs and talking to anybody she can find, including all the ships at sea . . . and Pud, of course.

"Say 'Calling WA6WXG, calling WA6WXG,' " she told me. "But don't say 'This is Andy.' I'll know. And if you lose the paper, remember it this way—Watch All Six Weasels Xing Geary. Geary Street, you know. But don't put the *S* for street on."

I nodded, and she did, too.

"Then slide the bar down and I'll come in. We'll be loud and clear because you're high up here and I am, too. There's nothing to block the signal."

She stared across at the bedside table with its white phone. "You can't use that even in an emergency, can you?"

"Uh uh," I said. "No way. The assistant manager would be up here in two minutes flat."

I clipped the Easi-Talkie onto my belt. "It's really nice of you to lend it to me, Leah."

"Yeah. Well, don't mess with it any. Those things are expensive. That one was for my birthday *and* Christmas."

"I know." I pulled my sweatshirt down to cover it and I felt like a cop with a gun, or at least a security guard. It was good that it was small and hardly showed.

"You can borrow it till you come home," Leah said.

"I'm not coming home," I reminded her. "I'm going to England."

"Oh, yeah, I forgot. Well, you can mail it back, then." Leah began packing the stuff back into the red-and-yellow bag. I couldn't see her face. "Are you sure you want to go to your dad?" she asked at last.

"If I can get the money." For some strange reason the ad for the ginger cat eased into my mind and with it came an excitement and the flash of an idea that vanished before I could grab it. The ginger cat and the three-hundred-dollar reward.

Leah stuck the Velcro straps shut. "Your mom and Paul stopped by our apartment today on their way back from the police station. That's how I know so much. Your mom looked awful. She had these big black rings under her eyes, like she hadn't slept."

I took one of my Superman laces from my pocket and began winding it around my thumb. Leah waited for me to say something and when I didn't she said, "My dad asked her if she was OK, and she said 'Not really,' and then he asked her why she'd waited a whole day before she went to the police. She said . . . she said you took some money." Leah pulled the Velcro open again. It sounded like a Band-Aid ripping off skin.

My face felt hot. "I only *borrowed* the money. To help pay for my plane fare. My dad'll send it back."

"Anyway, because you'd taken the money your mom was pretty sure you'd just run away. She thought you'd be back before night, because it's so scary in the city at night. But you weren't, and she and Paul went looking, cruising around, and then by this morning—"

"After breakfast," I added nastily.

"Whenever. She decided something awful could have happened. It's so hairy out on the streets." Leah glanced up at me. "So that's when they decided to go to the police."

"The police probably thought she was nuts. Kids run away all the time."

"Uh uh. They said they take it real seriously when a kid's twelve or under. They said you could possibly have been kidnapped, even."

I snorted. "Sure! Who'd want to kidnap me?"

"They say a kid twelve or under's called a critical missing and they pull out all the stops."

I took a deep breath and lay on my back on the rug watching the clock figures change on the ceiling. "I'll be thirteen next month, and I'll still be missing. Then they can start calling me something else. I guess I'll be spending my birthday with my dad."

"Your mom's awful worried, Andy. I almost told her because—"

I sat up again. "Whose side are you on? She lied to me. If she'd let me go to Dad, the way we arranged . . ."

Leah ran her fingers along a yellow stripe of the backpack. "She said he didn't want you to go. He called and said so."

"That's the story she gave me, too." The Superman shoelace was still around my thumb, and I pulled on it till it bit into my skin.

Mom had told me on Friday. I'd come in from school and found she was home early from work. "He says it's best if you don't go this summer, Andy. He's going to be busy out at the site and—"

"But he's always busy out at the site. In his letter he said I could come on the dig with him. He said there are lots of kids around who . . ."

Mom's face got tight. "What he told you in the letter and what he told me on the phone were two different things, Andy."

"When did he call?"

"This morning, after you left for school. I asked him to call back this afternoon. I said we'd call him. He told me he wouldn't be there. I said I'd go get you out of class so he could tell you himself. He said, 'No. Just you carry on, love.' His words." She gripped the edges of the kitchen table. "I wish he'd do his own dirty work. It's time I told you the way it really is, Andy. I'm tired of being the heavy all the time."

"Are you sure he even called?" I'd asked and she'd said, "Oh for heaven's sake, Andy. Why would I lie to you?"

"Because!" I'd run out of the kitchen and banged the door.

My thumb began to tingle, and I loosened the Superman lace. "She just doesn't want me and Dad to be together," I told Leah. "Remember, I was supposed to go for a whole two months last year and she said then . . ." I stopped and began rewinding the lace around my thumb.

"Maybe he was busy last year, too." Leah glanced up at me, and there was something in her face, some softness I'd seen before. It was the same sorry-for-you look Mrs. Saint had had this morning.

"It doesn't mean he doesn't want you *ever*," Leah went on. "Next summer . . ."

The elevator chimed.

"Sh!" I put my hand on her arm. "Quick! Somebody's coming."

I slid the backpack under the bed and wiggled after it. "Come on."

Leah's breathing was loud and scared beside me. We lay on our stomachs, facing each other.

Someone was coming into the bedroom, singing softly under her breath. I recognized the white, comfortable shoes. Mamie.

Leah had her eyes closed tight, as if that would make her invisible. Her face was all screwed up. I couldn't hear her heart thumping, but I could sure hear mine.

Mamie walked briskly into the bathroom where Leah and I'd been doing our mirror routine not ten minutes ago. Criminy! What if she'd come then?

I touched Leah's arm, and her eyes flicked open. "Mamie," I mouthed.

Mamie was coming back into the bedroom now. Her feet stopped at one of the damp spots on the rug, and she bent over to feel it. I saw the side of her face, her black hair pulled back, one silver hoop of an earring.

She straightened and made a little clicking sound that told me the damp spot didn't look all that great to her. She made the same sound when she inspected the drape. "That Fred sure is lazy," she muttered. I heard her go into the living room. Thank goodness I'd been smart enough to put the newspaper back.

A couple of seconds later I heard a chime and the whine of the elevator going down.

It took Leah and me a while to come out from under the shell bed. When we did, she stood, staring up at me.

"Whew!" I said, trying to smile. "Close one."

"Are you crazy?" she asked. "This place isn't safe."

"Sure it is." I hoped I sounded and looked courageous. "It'll only be for a while. Till I get in touch with Dad."

Leah glanced nervously in the direction of the elevator. "Are you sure she's gone?"

"She's gone."

"Look, Andy. This hideout isn't so great. Why don't you just come home?"

"No way," I said.

"Well, come hide under *my* bed. Honest. My mom never cleans under there. We could shovel it out so it wouldn't be too gross and we could bribe Parker to keep quiet. I know, we'll give him your baseball cards. He'd do anything for those cards. It's dumb to stay here."

"I'm staying," I said.

"Well, I'm not. And don't bother to ask me back. If you had a brain, you'd come with me. You're going to get caught."

"No, I'm not," I said. But I had a sinking feeling in my stomach. A lot of the time I don't listen to Leah. But a lot of the time she turns out to be right.

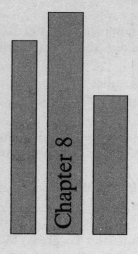

Chapter 8

Leah and I walked down five floors.

"These stairs are creepy," she whispered, and I nodded, not even liking the sound of the whisper in the deep concrete well that seemed to fall into emptiness below.

I stopped before I pushed open the door marked Thirtieth Floor.

"Will you give the High-Five Promise that you won't tell where I am?" I asked. "Even if the police come?"

Leah frowned. "I don't know if I want to promise."

"Please," I said, and she pulled at her tuft of hair, then said "OK" in a grumpy sort of way.

Our hands met at full stretch above our heads and our fingers locked. We'd started the High-Five Promise in third grade and kept a million promises together since, so I knew she'd never break it.

We walked together along the corridor to the elevator, but decided I shouldn't go down. The least times, the least risk.

"I'll write to you from England," I told her just as the elevator came. Then I patted my waist where the Easi-Talkie was hidden and added, "Watch All Six Weasels Xing Geary."

Leah nodded. "Roger."

The two women in the elevator smiled. They probably thought this was a secret code—kid stuff. If only they knew.

The doors closed and there was that faint whine, then silence. Leah had gone.

I walked along the hallway. A few late lunch or early dinner trays waited outside doors, and I checked to make sure the coast was clear, then investigated under the napkins.

I found half of a turkey sandwich and a bag of potato chips. On another tray was a frosted brownie all covered with Saran Wrap. Almost as good as Fred's mousse cake, I thought. Man, a guy could exist forever in this hotel. Or at least until he could get to England.

It was four-thirty when I got back to the Tower Suite.

I sat close to my bed escape route and ate what I'd taken from the trays. Good room service, I thought. And I still had my reserve supplies in the backpack.

By the time I'd finished eating I'd made a decision. I wouldn't wait three weeks for Dad to get back. I'd get the money myself, and I'd head straight for the Thames Valley. It was a famous excavation. Everybody would know where it was. I'd bypass Adpar Street where Dad wasn't and go where he was. I'd hitch into the dig site, or walk, and there he'd be. He'd look up and say, "Strike me pink if it isn't my son, Andrew. How are you, old sport? Got here on your own, did you? Bully for you."

He might even hug me.

I closed my eyes and I could see him in the picture he'd sent me a couple of years ago, wearing those too long shorts and that unbuttoned shirt, smiling his squinty-eyed smile. I tried hard to see him working, digging, I guess, but he kept turning into Paul Paws, spading out a hole for the lemon tree or turning over the earth for the seeds of springtime. Dad turning into Paul Paws really bugged me.

But . . . how was I going to get the money? How?

I tried to bring back the flash of the idea that had almost come when I'd read about the ginger cat with the three-hundred-dollar reward. And there was something else, too, something Leah had said. I knew there was a connection. But both thoughts had gone.

I'm not sure when they came back, though I think it was the cat one that came first. It didn't come while

I was in the bathroom splashing water over my face, carefully drying the sink when I'd finished. I'd thought if I had a towel I could take a shower, but I couldn't. It was too dangerous. If someone came while I was in the shower, in the bathroom even, there'd be no place to hide. I'd be there reflected a hundred times over in those mirrors. I got out as fast as possible.

The cat idea didn't come again while I was changing clothes, either, pulling up those giant shorts of Leah's dad. They kept falling down, but I tightened my belt and hitched them out over the waistband of my jeans and that worked pretty well. I put on the mustard sweatshirt, pulled it down to cover the top of the shorts and the Easi-Talkie, slid my bare feet into my shoes, and stuffed everything else in the backpack. And all the time that cat and whatever Leah had said chased each other inside my head. I knew it wasn't the cat himself that was important here. It was that they'd pay to get him back.

It was while I was eating one of Leah's Oreos, my hand carefully cupped beneath it to catch the crumbs, that I remembered both and how they went together. I almost choked. Crazy thoughts raced around inside my head. Would it work? Wait, I needed paper and pencil. I needed to get this straight.

The bowlegged desk in the corner had engraved Countess International stationery and cards and a silver pen on a stand. I took the pen and a card, and sat on the floor by the bed.

It was 5:22 and the light wasn't great so far from the windows, but there was enough.

I made a list of the things I'd have to get, sucking the end of the silver pen, imagining how it would be, my stomach getting a horrible feeling. Could I do it? Look, I told myself, do it and you'll have the money. You'll get out of here. It will be all over.

Six things on the list. Too late to get them tonight. I'd go out in the morning early, so I'd be sure to miss Mamie, and I'd buy what I needed. They'd be good investments. Wait, one of them might be here in the room. I could check it out right now.

Yeah! The round white sewing basket on the dresser had small scissors in it. I took them out, ran the edge of my finger along the blades, then put them back. They'd be here tomorrow when I needed them. So that was one thing I could take off the list.

And there was something else I might be able to get tonight.

I stowed the backpack carefully under the bed and went back through the Tower Suite lobby.

Mamie's flowers looked as fresh as ever, reflecting pink in the mirror that reflected me, too, my hair sleek and wet, the neckband of the mustard sweatshirt dark where water had soaked it. I squinted my eyes the way Dad's had been in the photograph. Did I look like him? Maybe.

The door to the stairs always made a clicking sound when it closed, but by now I knew it and eased the door gently shut behind me.

Down to thirty-three this time. Smart to make a change. Safer.

Here was the other door marked Private, the one right next to the stairs, the same on every floor. I opened it cautiously. Nobody inside, just the smells of bleach and cleanser and floor wax. I didn't dare switch on the light, and I had to stand for a minute getting my eyes used to the dark before feeling my way along the shelves. After a moment, I could see a muddle of rubber gloves thrown in a careless pile. I stuffed two into my jeans pockets. After I used them, I'd put them back as easily as I'd borrowed them, and no one would know.

Out and along the corridor to the elevator.

A woman and a man, all dressed up, came from one of the rooms and walked behind me.

"What time are we meeting the Valentinos?" the man asked.

"Seven-thirty," the woman said.

I guessed they were going to some fancy place to eat, maybe even the famous one with the singing waiters where Mom and Paul Paws had gone on their six month anniversary.

"I didn't know people celebrated six months," I'd said nastily.

The woman and man weren't friendly like the

83

Saints. We didn't talk as we waited for the elevators. They went down in one, and I went up in another, and in a few seconds I was back in the Tower Suite.

I stored the gloves in the backpack and crossed them off my list.

Four things left, and nothing I could do about those till morning.

I sat on the floor close to the bed, unclipped the Easi-Talkie, and pushed the slide up so I could talk.

"Calling WA6WXG. Calling WA6WXG." At first I forgot to pull it back down so I could hear, and there was nothing. But then I remembered and did, and right away Leah's voice came on.

"This is WA6WXG. Come in."

I could hardly believe it. It was as clear as talking on a phone.

"How are you?" I asked. "What's happening?" Dumb, but I couldn't think of anything else to say. Certainly not, "I've got the gloves, I've got the scissors, pretty soon I'll be on my way."

I pulled down the slide.

"Those people I told you about came," Leah said. "But I High-Fived."

"Thanks. I mean it."

"Fortunately, Parker was at the Y having his swimming lesson. I don't know if I could have kept him from blabbing. Any problems on your end?"

"No. I'm about to hit the sack. I'm real tired."

There was a pause, and then Leah said, "Be careful."

"I will."

I had the list in front of me. She could probably get some of these other things for me if I asked, but she'd want to know why, and I couldn't tell her why. She'd try to stop me.

I could imagine her voice. "You're going to do *what?* That's the rottenest thing I ever heard in my life."

It was. But the police were looking for me. I needed money. I was desperate.

"You think those are reasons?" she'd ask. "You're sick, Andy. *S-i-c-k.*" She might even feel she had to tell "those people."

"Well," I said. "I guess this is it for now. Goodnight."

"Goodnight," Leah said. "Over and out."

It was six-forty. I'd hardly slept last night what with Fred and Baby and being so nervous. And now I couldn't sleep either because my mind was jazzed up with excitement and fear. My stomach heaved.

Did I dare turn on the bedroom TV? Without sound, maybe, so I could keep listening for that give-away chime of the elevator?

I practiced getting from the TV back to the bed. The clock told me it took two seconds to turn off the set and close the cabinet doors, another six to get to my hiding place. I could do it if I had to, and I probably wouldn't have to. Mamie would have gone home hours ago.

I set the volume as low as it would go and pulled

the On knob. There was a rerun of a movie that I'd already seen. I could almost lip-read, I remembered it so well. I also remembered that Mom and I'd watched it together, sitting on the couch with our feet on the coffee table, crunching the popcorn she'd made.

She'd cried at the end, soundlessly, the way she does, the way she did when Dad left. Leah says maybe that's when Mom learned to cry so quietly, so I wouldn't hear and be too upset, because I was just a little kid of seven at the time. But sometimes I'd heard anyway.

I jumped up and switched off the TV set before the ending could come, but I felt as sad as if I'd seen it. Now my chest heaved, too.

"Don't be such a baby," I said out loud. "You're going to do this, so cut out the mushy stuff."

It was 8:53.

I crept into the living room and swiveled the telescope up to the night sky. Paul Paws says if you feel bad, go out and look at the stars. "They're always there, even if you can't see them, even in the daytime." He'd smiled at me. "They're like love, Andy."

If he was trying to tell me something meaningful, I didn't get it.

Tonight the sky was low and filled with darkness, and though I turned the telescope in every direction, I couldn't find a single star.

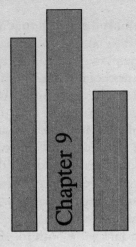

Chapter 9

By two the next afternoon I'd been out and was already safely back in the Tower Suite. Knowing the police were looking for me made everything harder. I'd seen enough TV to know about the bulletins they put out to patrol cars when they're trying to find someone. Maybe every cop in the city had a computer picture of me by now. The critical missing! I'd pulled the hood of the mustard sweatshirt around my face and walked fast.

There was something I invested in that wasn't on my list. At a stall in front of a small shop on Market Street, I'd found a long, dark blue sweatshirt that I'd changed into right away. It made me feel more anonymous than when I was wearing Leah's Special Sneak Preview. It also came well down over the top of her dad's underpants that bunched like a pale blue frill around my middle. It hid the Easi-Talkie clipped to my belt.

Before I started work on the plan, I ate four slices of the bread and some of the luncheon meat. Mamie had been there, all right, so I could relax a bit. Today's newspapers were in the living room, and the silver fruit bowl had been refilled. There were wonderful looking nectarines and peaches right on top. The sweet, ripe smell of the peaches drifted my direction as I tiptoed past, but there were only four of them, and for all I knew, Mamie kept count. I was hungry, but I left the fruit where it was.

The rubber gloves I'd picked up were both for the right hand but I turned one of them inside out. On the rug by the bed I spread the newspaper I'd bought, got the scissors, and began searching for the words I needed.

The paper was the kind you see next to supermarket checkout counters, the kind filled with far-out stories.

I'd bought glue, a yellow lined pad, and a Hallmark card in the same little market.

It wasn't easy working with the small sewing scissors, my fingers covered with thick rubber gloves which were too big to begin with. But I had to. "No fingerprints," I'd warned Leah when she'd been here and leaned close to the mirror. "Mamie might see."

I had to be even more careful about fingerprints now. Super careful.

I made myself work tidily and slowly as I snipped

out the words, gathering the extra scraps of paper as I went in case I heard that warning elevator chime.

There was one problem I'd been wrestling with in the night and this morning, too. I left a blank space for it as I lined the cutout words in front of me, making my sentences. "Worth" was the hardest one to find. I finally spotted it in a diet ad. "What is it worth to you to have a model figure? Try our Slim Quick diet." It was a good thing Mom changed her name when she married. And that was the first time I'd ever had *that* thought. *Winfield* was easy. *Dubin* I'd have had to make from separate letters.

I had the whole message now, except for the blank, and there'd have to be a decision on that pretty soon.

The stopper was stuck in the glue bottle even though it was new and I had to wrestle it off so I could stick the words on the yellow paper. Then they kept sticking to my gloved hands instead, as if they didn't want to put themselves on the paper.

I HAVE YOUR SON. HE WILL BE SAFE IF YOU PAY   . PUT MONEY UNDER LEFT FOOT OF ST. FRANCIS IN PEPPERTREE PARK AT 11 P.M. TUESDAY. DO NOT CALL POLICE. I WILL BE WATCHING.

The cutout words in different shapes and sizes almost filled the yellow page, running in uneven lines.

I did the envelope.

MRS. WINFIELD
3I2 WORTH STREET
SAN FRANCISCO

The zip numbers came from the sports page, too, where I'd found *win* and *field*.

For the first time I looked at the card that I'd taken from the envelope. It had a sad-eyed sheep on the front. The message inside said, Aw C'mon. Let's Be Friends Again.

The card almost freaked me out. I'd bought it because the envelope was the biggest one on the rack, and I'd figured I'd toss the card. But when I looked at that sad-eyed sheep, I thought I'd keep it and send it to Mom afterward, from England, when all this was over.

Yeah, sure. And Mom would forgive me just because I sent a cute card. Get real, Andy. But I wrapped it carefully in paper before I slid it into the backpack, just in case.

How much money should I put in the blank? I would need four hundred dollars or so for the airline ticket. That's what it was when I checked the Super Saver last time. Whatever was left of my own reserve I'd have to keep for England because I might need to get a bus or train from the airport. But four hundred dollars didn't seem like what a kidnapper would ask for. If Barnstable's owner was offering three hundred dollars, it should be a lot more for a person.

I looked at the blank space till the letters ran together in a blur. How about five hundred dollars? Would she have that much? I didn't want to worry her too much. Dealing with a son who'd been kidnapped would be hard enough without having to rush around borrowing money. In the end it wouldn't matter how much I got because I'd send it all back. . . . Dad would. Plus what I'd taken from Paul Paws. I'd put it in an envelope with the sheep card and I'd write how desperate I'd been, and how I hoped I hadn't scared her too much, and that she might not believe it, but that I loved her. My love was like the stars, there even when you couldn't see it. It was just—I had to go.

My eyes began to sting.

"But why did you have to go, Andy?" she'd ask.

"Because you don't care about me anymore. You used to. But now you have Paul Paws and you don't need me." Saying it out loud like that made it true. It was true. But still, I wished I hadn't said it.

"Do you think your dad needs you?" she'd ask.

I jumped up. Why was I thinking stuff like this? Mom couldn't ask me questions, could she? She wouldn't be there. I walked round and round the Tower Suite, taking deep gulpy breaths. Then I went back, dragged out the discarded pieces of paper, and searched for more words to tack on the bottom.

P.S. YOUR KID SAYS HE LOVES YOU.

I folded the yellow paper and slid it into the envelope. After it got dark I'd go to our house and put it in the mailbox or even under the door. No use mailing it because that could take forever, and I didn't have forever. I'd have to be extra careful, though, because the police might have a stakeout. I'd have to be real clever and sneaky.

It was 4:48. Leah would be home from school.

I unclipped the Easi-Talkie from my belt. "Calling WA6WXG. Calling WA6WXG."

She answered immediately. "Don't say your name. Are you OK?"

I made myself sound real cheerful. "Sure. Why wouldn't I be?"

There was silence for a few seconds before she asked, "Have you seen today's *Chronicle?*"

I glanced toward the door. The *Chronicle* would be in the living room with all the other papers. "No," I said. "Why?"

"You should look at it," Leah said. "It's very interesting."

"OK, I'm going. Over and out."

And there I was on the second page. The picture of me was small, not even baseball card size. It was the school one from last year when my hair was longer. The write-up was short:

"Andy Dubin, twelve years old, missing from home since Saturday morning. Andy is just over five feet tall and weighs 84 lbs. He has light brown hair

92

and blue eyes. He is believed to be wearing jeans, a Forty Niners sweatshirt over a white T-shirt, white Reebok tennis shoes with Superman laces. Anyone with information is asked to contact the San Francisco Police Department."

Oh, criminy, I thought. Now it's not only the police who have my picture. It's everyone who reads the *Chronicle* and notices. Of course, the photograph's not very big, and I'm not wearing the Forty Niners shirt or the laces anymore. But it might be bigger—tomorrow—when they find out about the kidnapping.

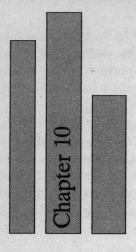

Chapter 10

I watched the clock. 5:55.

I'd take the letter to our house at about eleven. Eleven seemed a good time, not late enough to be totally scary; late enough so the police, if there were any around, might be sleepy and not as sharp as usual. Dark enough so anyone who'd seen that picture wouldn't recognize me.

I watched all the evening news programs without sound, switching channels, looking nervously for myself but never finding me. Not important enough for television. Not yet.

Mom wouldn't get the note till morning, probably. Paul Paws would see it when he went out to bring in the paper and the rose that he always brings in for her. The way he picks those roses, you'd think his bush would be bald by now. Mom would read it and start to cry in that silent, hurting way. She'd put her hands over her mouth to stop the sounds that weren't there.

I paced round and round the Tower Suite. After a while I began to feel like I was on one of those moving belts where you walk and never get anywhere. They have one at the Children's Museum.

I stared at the statue of St. Francis through the telescope, imagining Mom sitting where I'd sat, feeling for the gap under the big, stone foot. She'd have to squeeze hard to get the money to fit into the space. Five hundred dollars would be thick. Unless maybe they were all fifties or hundreds. I've never seen a hundred-dollar bill. Maybe Paul Paws would bring the money. For sure he'd be with her. He always goes with her when she has to do something hard, like the time she had the tests in the hospital. Dad sure left Mom to face a lot of hard things alone. It was a traitor thought, and I squashed it away fast.

So Mom and Paul Paws would both come, and I'd be up here in my hideout, watching.

A black-and-white police car came sliding around the park. Through the telescope, I saw the two officers inside. One of them was wearing wraparound dark glasses. His head turned in my direction and I ducked back, which was silly because of course he couldn't see me, no way. But I felt sort of sick, anyway.

10:10. I swept the telescope across the bay, over

the span of the bridge with its moving bands of red and white car lights, people coming into the city, people heading out. There were so many stars that the sky looked milky. I picked out the Big Dipper hanging over Alcatraz Island.

10:16. I'd wait five minutes more. I'd call Leah, call for the last time. She wouldn't want to talk to me after she found out what I'd done. And anyway, I'd be gone.

She came on right away, as if she'd been waiting.

"We went over to your house tonight after dinner," she said. "My mom took cookies she'd baked. Oatmeal raisin."

"Oh?"

"Your mom was wearing her blue skirt, the one that flares out and has flowers around the bottom. You know, the one you like? But she looked scary, Andy, all white and trembly. Paul says she's close to the edge, whatever that means."

I nibbled at my thumbnail. "How come she was all dressed up? Was she going dancing or something?"

"Don't be sarcastic, OK? You know she's not going dancing."

I didn't answer and Leah went, "Hello? Hello? Are you there?"

"I'm here."

"She was wearing your diamond bow in her hair." Leah sounded like she was accusing me of something, just because Mom was wearing her diamond bow. "She said she wanted to look nice, in case you came home."

I took a deep breath. "I have to go, OK? Over and out."

"Wait, wait . . ." I cut her off and sat looking at the Easi-Talkie, feeling that chokiness in my throat. I'd have to get this back to Leah somehow. So Mom was dressed up and wearing my bow. So what? I had to stick to my plan.

10:21. I dragged my backpack from under the bed and took out the ransom note. I still hadn't sealed the envelope. I slid out the folded yellow paper. It was too dark to read the words, but I didn't need to because I knew them. I'd probably know them forever. And then the strangest thing happened. I discovered I was crying, soundlessly the way Mom does. See, I thought, wiping my eyes with the backs of my hands. See? I don't cry like Dad, I cry like you. Did Dad cry? I didn't know. Did he cry when he left us? If he did, no one saw. I know Mom cried when she told me he'd gone.

"His work means more to him than anything, Andy. It's his life. I've tried to fight that for both you and me. The fight's over."

"But why, Mom?"

"Because we couldn't win. I accepted that in the end."

Why was I remembering these things now? Why

was I remembering the sadness in Jean's faraway London voice? Was she losing the fight, too?

It was 10:33. I clipped on the Easi-Talkie, pulled the sweatshirt down, and slid the note carefully into my jeans pocket. I fastened the backpack Velcro. Tonight I'd come back here, but tomorrow, early, I'd have to split forever. No hanging around. Too many fingers to point to this hotel if Mom told about the kidnap. There'd been that description of me already. If they blew up my picture, put it on the front page, lots of people would remember for sure.

10:35. I had to get out of here.

I sat on the edge of the long pink chair trying to make myself move, but my insides ached as if I'd been kicked in the stomach. Mom's face drifted in and out of my mind. The diamond bow that I'd bought for her, the one that wasn't made of diamonds at all, glittered as bright as the tears on her cheeks had the day I'd given it to her.

"Happy birthday," I'd said. It was way back, BPP and AD. Maybe I was eight. "Here. These are real diamonds." I'd sent away for it. Fabulous Diamond Hair Clip. Unbelievably Low Price. $5.95 plus $1.25 postage.

"It's beautiful," she'd said, hugging me tight, clipping it in her tawny hair, except that then I didn't know her hair was tawny. "I'll wear it forever. But only on very special occasions."

She'd worn it on Easter Sundays and every Christmas and when we went out for dinner on birthdays. Even when some of the diamonds fell out. Even when the clip rusted. She'd worn it the day she married Paul Paws. She was wearing it now, waiting for me to come home. Probably she'd waited for Dad to come home. Now it was me. I felt myself crying again, and I knew I couldn't hurt her this badly. It had been some kind of game up till now, a game to punish Mom for leaving me for Paul Paws. But she hadn't left me. Dad had. She was waiting.

"I'm not leaving, Mom," I said out loud. "You'll see, I'm not like Dad that way. You don't have to worry."

It was incredible how light I felt suddenly, light as a leaf drifting down from a cherry tree. I'd take a cab home. I'd never ridden in a cab before, and I had enough of my own money left for that. I'd cab it right up to our door and . . .

Sh! What was that? The elevator chime.

I grabbed the backpack and dived under the bed.

But why was I so scared? I was coming out of hiding anyway, wasn't I? Though if this was the police I'd be in a lot of trouble. I'd probably broken a bunch of laws. And suppose it was somebody else?

I lay, scrunched as small as I could make myself under the bed.

No sound. But a small sense told me someone had gone into the living room. No voices. One person maybe. Didn't cops travel in pairs? No footsteps, but how could there be on these thick rugs? Had the living room lights gone on? I couldn't tell.

The bedroom door opened, a flashlight beam, a big one, dark feet and legs behind it. The whiteness of light raced across the rug. It stopped in front of the closet. Boots, a man's boots, chunky with brass chains or something looped at the ankles followed it. The closet doors slid back, closed silently again—now the doors to the balcony. I lay motionless as a sleeping alligator.

The booted feet came in again, coming toward the bed, stopping.

Leah's backpack was slippery under my hands. My heart was ready to explode.

The pink frill on the bottom of the bedspread twitched up so that there was space, filled with the blinding glare of the flashlight. I squinched my eyes shut, opened them, tried to shade them against the brightness. I'd never been so frightened in my life. Someone, dark and shadowy. A voice, dark and shadowy, too. "Out," it said. "Out."

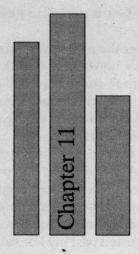

Chapter 11

I crawled out, blinded by the light.

A hand yanked me to my feet, and the voice said, "I thought so," and then, "I see you dumped the Forty Niners shirt and those cool-out shoelaces."

"Fred!" I said. "But you don't have a key. You gave Mamie's back." What a stupid dweebish thing to say, but it was the first thing that tripped into my mind.

"Ever hear of getting a duplicate?" he asked. "That's when you take the key into a lock shop and . . ."

"I know how it's done." I shook my arm. "Let go!" I was trying to sound tough, but I could tell I wasn't making it.

Fred sounded tough all right. "No way. What else

have you got under that bed? Get it out." He gave me a push.

"OK, OK." I wriggled under the pink cover, past the backpack, and made a quick crawling bolt to the other side. I'd taken maybe three steps toward the door when Fred caught me. The flashlight beam danced crazily on the ceiling. I kicked at his legs, got one hand free, and pushed toward his face.

He held my wrists. "Take it easy. All I'm going to do is take you back to your parents. Or do you want me to call the cops instead? You'd be in real trouble then." My arms were pinned behind me now, and Fred had somehow turned me so my back was toward him. A smell of garlic gusted past my left ear. "How does breaking and entering sound to you?" he asked.

"I didn't," I said.

"Trespassing. Maybe stealing a little here and there, for all I know?"

"I *didn't*," I said again, but I wasn't certain. I'd taken Paul Paws's money, and the food off the trays, and the gloves that I still hadn't put back.

"Or I could call one of the managers," Fred said. "It's up to you." I could feel the heat of him. The garlic smell was disgusting.

"But why do you want to take me home? I don't get it."

I felt him shrug. "I wouldn't mind being a hero. Besides, when I ran away maxi-years ago, my old

102

lady offered a nice reward to anybody who returned her lost lamb. Nobody did. But people are sentimental about their kids. They're generous—a time or two—till they get fed up." His grip tightened. "I hope your old lady isn't fed up yet."

"No," I said. "I don't think so." Then I added, "I'm not real sure she'd give a reward, though."

"We'll see. Now get the bag from under the bed. We can't trash up the Tower Suite."

He shone the light for me, and I dragged out Leah's backpack.

"OK. Now we'll go down the emergency stairs and pick up the service elevator. Where do you live, kid? Somewhere in the city?"

"Worth Street," I said.

He nodded. "I know where it's at."

The stair door made its usual click as Fred closed it behind us. In the overhead light, for the first time I really saw him; he wasn't the way I'd imagined him, with a ratty face and a pointed chin. He had a round head and face and dimples that were there even when he wasn't smiling, like now. His hair was dark and long, straggling over the collar of his worn leather jacket. He wasn't tall, but his shoulders bulged under the leather. No wonder he'd had no trouble holding me. A white silky scarf was knotted at his neck, the fringed ends hanging down.

He was looking at me, too. "You did OK, kid, finding a place like this. You made just one little mistake." He pointed down. "You got rid of those funky laces too late. The minute I read about them, I remembered the mysterious shoes in the Tower Suite, and I had a hunch who they belonged to."

We were going down the concrete steps now, me in front, his hand on my shoulder. This wasn't the way I wanted it to end. I didn't want somebody bringing me back like a lost package. I'd wanted Mom to know it was my own choice, that I couldn't bear to hurt her anymore. Being brought was awful. Maybe I could . . .

I swung the backpack by its straps as hard as I could against Fred's stomach and began pelting down the stairs. Down and down, round and round, no sound except the rattle of my own breathing, Fred's boots clattering behind me. Down and down, round and round, slipping, skidding, falling. The door of the thirty-second floor. If I got through it, along the corridor, into the elevator . . .

His hands pressed down on my shoulders so that I sprawled on one of the steps. He threw the backpack beside me and gave that bad-tempered grunt that I remembered from the night with Baby.

"All right, that's *it*," he said. "I'm calling the cops. Now."

"No." My chest was heaving so much I could hardly get the word out. "Please. I won't try anything else."

"You'd better not." He was scowling, the scowl

deepening his dimples so his face had holes in it. "This is your last chance. I'm warning you."

"I won't run again. Honest."

He pushed open the door to the thirty-second floor. "If we meet anyone, act normal. And don't say a word. That way you'll get home faster."

We met two men with Artisans and Engineers Conference badges on. They didn't even look at us as we passed.

The service elevator was at the back of the utility room. It was a metal box with no carpeting and no mirrors and it smelled of disinfectant. And Fred's garlic. It was slow, too. We didn't talk or look at each other on the way down.

The service exit led onto a dark side street where cars were parked, nose to tail. Fred stopped at a van. I guessed it was the one I'd seen Baby and him get into when I'd watched through the telescope, though it was hard to be sure in the dark.

"What number on Worth?" he asked.

"Three-twelve."

He opened one of the back doors and stood behind me as I climbed into the darkness. I thought he'd leave me then and go get in the front, but he jumped in beside me and switched on a small light. The van floor was carpeted in the kind of rough matting you find around swimming pools. The small windows on the side and the oval one in back were covered with black paper. There was an unrolled sleeping bag, a surfboard on a rack, and on the other side a small red motorbike fastened with metal rails to the floor.

"I'm going to be driving," he said. "And it's not that I don't trust you, you understand? But let's have a look at what you've got in that backpack."

I began pulling things out. "Not much," I said. "There's this sweatshirt, and this one, and this pad of paper, and . . ."

Fred took the bag and emptied it onto the floor. The chain on his boot swung and jingled as he used his foot to sort through my underwear, socks, towel, the empty can of luncheon meat, the cheese and bread and cookie wrappers, the rubber gloves, the glue, the card, the tangled Superman laces, the key. The newspaper scraps left over from the ransom note fluttered down.

"What *is* this?" Fred asked. "Were you making a rat's nest?"

I shrugged and pulled down my sweatshirt.

Fred picked up the key and put it in his pocket, touched his toe to the laces. "Ah, yes. The big giveaway . . ." His smile brought out his dimples again and made his eyes disappear.

"Let's check your pockets, too. You don't have one of those tricky little Boy Scout knives hidden away? Or some other lethal weapon?"

"No," I said. "Honest."

I took out Mr. Saint's business card and put it on

the rug. Beside it I piled what was left of the money. "You could take this to pay for gas," I said, knowing what else was in my pocket, hoping and hoping Fred wouldn't see it. Why hadn't I torn that awful ransom note into little pieces and flushed it down the soundless toilet? He'd come in too fast, that was why. But if he showed this to Mom, she'd know what I'd been planning, and she'd look at me, so horrified, so sick, that I'd want to die.

Fred was counting the money. "What did you do? Rob a bank?"

"No. I took it from home. Borrowed it, so I could go to my dad's, in England."

"Uh-HUH!" He folded the money and slid it into some inside pocket. "Do you have a passport?"

"What?"

"You know, the little book with your mug shot inside. The one they stamp." He closed a fist and thumped it a few times into his other palm.

"I know what a passport is," I muttered, and Fred smiled.

"You ain't going no place without it, kid."

"I could have got one," I said.

"Sure you could."

I stood there, feeling stupid and hopeless. All this, and the ransom note, and I couldn't have gone to England anyway.

"Any pockets in that sweatshirt?" I shook my head. "Well, turn out your jeans pockets."

"But . . ."

"Just do it."

I tugged them out, squinting down at the little bits of fluff and Kleenex stuck in the seams, trying to hide the ransom note in my hand. "See?" I said. "Nothing else."

He saw it. "What's that? Give it here."

I reached it toward him and quick grabbed it with my other hand. I tried to rip it but he snatched it away.

"You are not a very cooperative kid—did anyone ever tell you that?"

I watched as he smoothed out the envelope, looked at it, then pulled out the yellow paper. His lips moved as he read. In the street outside, a car engine started. The bottom corner of the right hand window covering had been torn away and the car's headlights shone through, white and bright. Then it was dark again. Night traffic rumbled, low as faraway thunder.

At last Fred looked up.

"I've got to hand it to you, kid. You're pretty smart. If you were a bit smarter, though, you'd have asked for more money. Way more money."

"Mom doesn't have way more money. Anyway, I wasn't going to send it."

Fred tapped the note against his chin. "I'm not sure about that PS. It's a dead giveaway, but a major heartbreaker. I think that might have done it for you. She'd have coughed up the bucks for sure."

"I tell you, I wasn't going to send it."

He smiled. "Naw. You just put this together to pass the time." He put the note in his pocket. "Kid," he said. "I'm going to tell you something because I know. A lot of things start the day you decide to run away. And when they start they're real hard to stop."

And then, somehow, he'd moved fast as a snake, and I was facedown on the scratchy matting and he was tying my hands behind me. I kicked, scissoring my knees back, wriggling and squirming. But he was sitting on my legs now, grunting, pulling something tight around my ankles.

"Help!" I yelled. "Somebody help!"

My face scratched against the rug again, and something soft was forced into my mouth and tied behind my head.

Fred rolled me over onto my back.

"I have to think," he said. "I have to drive and think and not worry about you and whether you're trying to pull something back here. I'm not going to hurt you."

Standing over me he seemed huge, a giant with a monster shadow that lurched across the ceiling of the van, all dark hunched shoulders and round basketball head.

"You probably don't believe that, but it's true. I'm not into hurting kids. But you just gave me an idea. Why count on your old lady being grateful? This is a surer way to get what I want. We're going to drive up to a place I know. You just lie there and enjoy the ride."

He stepped over me and then across to the front of the van, pushing apart the dark divider curtains. He was gone. I was trembling. He was gone. And he'd missed something.

I saw his face one more time as he leaned back to click off the light.

I was in absolute darkness.

The van started on the second try. I felt us back up a little, then go forward. We were moving, going somewhere to a place he knew. He'd said he wouldn't hurt me. That's what he'd said.

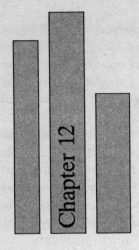

Chapter 12

I lay on my back in the dark, feeling every rattle and bump in my bones, my mind racing with fear.

Ever since I was little, Mom had warned me about getting into cars with strangers . . . to be careful with anybody. And here I was in a van, being kidnapped, probably. And I'd come willingly, walked right out and into the trap. Don't kids who get kidnapped usually end up . . . no! Don't think about that. It's hard enough to breathe now, but when you start thinking about what could happen you won't be able to breathe at all. Calm down. Calm. Try to think. But how could I think when my mind was slithering like this?

We made a sharp turn. The surfboard slid a little on the rack. The wheels of the motorbike turned.

The gag in my mouth smelled of aftershave or

cologne. Each time the van swayed, something like spiderwebs brushed across my face, and I realized Fred had used his scarf to gag me and that the spiderwebs were its fringed ends. I strained at my wrists, but whatever was holding them had no give at all. My ankles felt glued together, too.

For a while I tried counting the turns we made, the number of times we stopped, but it all muddled together. I tried to figure out if we were going north or south or east or west. There was no way to know. Through the torn corner I saw only darkness, sometimes slices of tall, lighted buildings. Had we been driving for an hour? Not that much, probably.

The smell of the matting made my nose itch. I sneezed and almost choked on the gag.

Fred's face poked through the curtain. "God bless," he said.

Were we slowing? Yes, but picking up speed again, quickly. There was a different surface under our wheels. *Ka-thump, ka-thump*, rough and rumbling, but regular. I'd felt this and heard it before. I raised my head. Through the tear I saw dimly lit poles, like a dull orange fence sliding past us. No, not poles, rust-colored cables, each one thick as an arm, and always that steady *ka-thump, ka-thump*.

I knew. I knew where we were. We were on the Golden Gate Bridge. Paul Paws and I'd crossed it on the night we went star watching on Mount Tamalpais, him talking about girders and beams and metal expansion, me slumped in cranky silence. What a jerk I'd been!

The orange cables weren't sliding past us now. I remembered that there was a steep hill that started where the bridge ended. I listened, tense and waiting, and heard Fred shift the van into low gear. I told myself that at least now I knew where we were. But knowing didn't make me feel much better.

The sudden blare of the radio made my heart leap. Above my head the back speaker spat out a jumble of voices, music, static. It settled on a news station. The reader was a woman, cheerful even as she told of a giant oil spill that was killing birds and seals by the hundreds. She gave sports scores, business news. Now and then she chirped the time.

"It's one-thirty A.M. and the temperature in the Bay Area is a cool, spicy forty-two degrees."

We'd been driving for an hour then, so we'd gone about fifty miles. Was that right?

I was glad Fred had switched on the radio; if I concentrated on what she was saying about somebody merging with somebody and about a guy trying to buy an airline, I couldn't hear my own thoughts so clearly.

And then two things happened. I found that the gag around my mouth was loosening. Silky, I thought. The knots are sliding. That's what happens to Mom when she wears that flowered scarf; it keeps coming untied. If I rub my head from side to side, I just bet

I could get this thing loose enough so I could spit it out and wriggle it down. I just bet I could!

I tried, then stopped. This wasn't the right time. When we got where we were going, Fred might check to see if everything was still OK, and I didn't want him tightening the scarf or finding something else to use. Something I'd never get out of. I'd lie and be patient and then, when he left me—because that's what I figured he'd do, leave me tied up—then I'd . . .

And then the second thing happened. I heard my name on the radio. "There is still no sign of twelve-year-old Andy Dubin, missing from his home since early Saturday morning. A spokesman for the SFPD does say, however, that they have several leads. A boy answering to Andy's description was seen in the vicinity of the Countess International Hotel. Witnesses report he was in the company of a middle-aged man and woman, since identified as guests in the hotel. A police spokesperson says the couple has been contacted but their identities have not been released. It is known, though, that they live in New Orleans and that they did have valuable information."

The Saints, I thought. Mr. and Mrs. Doug Ackerman. Oh, no. I hope nobody's suspecting them of kidnapping me! What was this valuable information they had? I imagined Mr. Saint telling the police, "The boy seemed worried about that stepfather of his. He told us the guy wasn't nice to him. Have you checked him out? He sounded like a no-good son-of-a-gun to me."

What if they suspected Paul Paws? I wished I hadn't said that. It wasn't even true. Paul was nice to me.

The van curtains parted, and the side of Fred's head poked through while he kept his eyes on the road.

"Let's keep the SFPD following those valuable leads in New Orleans. They've got no reason to check me." He disappeared, came back. "Good thing I got you out of that hotel. Those cops were hot on your trail."

Oh, sure, I thought. Great! As if I didn't wish I was in a police car right now on my way to the station to be charged with anything, instead of in Fred's van heading for who knew what.

I could tell we were climbing on a straight road. Loose things began rolling toward the back of the van. The motor shifted again into a lower gear. Gravel scrunched and rattled under the tires. We stopped and Fred turned off the engine.

Over the beating of my own heart, I could hear the hot tick-tock of the motor, loud as an alarm clock. Fred pulled aside the curtains. "We're here, kid."

He hopped into the back, switched on the dim lights, and squatted beside me. First he rolled me over to pull my wrist rope. Then he rolled me back and tugged on the one holding my ankles. For some reason he had a pencil stuck behind one ear.

Now he'd check the gag. I filled my mouth with all the air it could hold and bulged my cheek and neck muscles. Fred tried to poke a finger between the scarf and my face and couldn't.

"OK," he said.

I watched as he went to where the stuff had piled up by the back doors, found the yellow pad, and sat with his knees up. He fished my ransom note and envelope from his pocket and took the pencil from behind his ear.

"Let's see now," he muttered.

With the pad against his knees, he began to write on the first page of the pad, or print probably. I knew exactly what he was doing. He was writing his own ransom note.

"You didn't pick a good place for the drop off," he said. "You need somewhere less conspicuous, know what I mean? That park's got people around, day and night."

He stared at me blankly for a few seconds, then began to print again.

It was quite a while before he stuck the pencil back behind his ear. "I'm putting that PS in my version," he said. "I liked that."

"Mm oo oin oo et e eed t?" I mumbled, but he paid no attention. Of course he wasn't going to let me read it.

He examined the envelope. "Too bad you messed this up. But it'll do."

Now he was searching for something, toeing through my spilled stuff, pushing aside the two sweatshirts, the blue towel. "Aha!" he said, pouncing on the Superman laces.

Carefully he looped them inside the yellow paper and slid the note into the envelope.

"I guess your mom will know I've got the right kid all right," he said. "There can't be too many of these around."

He winked down at me, then patted my head. I tried to jerk away and that made him laugh. When he laughed his face stopped being round and turned into a football shape.

"Once I get the money, I'm turning you loose, Andy," he said.

Maybe my eyes showed what I was thinking.

"No, I will," he said. "That's a promise. You just lie here and ponder your evil ways while I'm gone. Just think, if you hadn't come up with this kidnapping plan I might not have thought of it. Of course, I might have. I'm usually good for an idea or two myself if there's quick money in it." He put the envelope in the pocket of the leather jacket and zipped it safely inside.

The motorbike lifted easily out of the two chrome clips. He kicked the mess out of the way and opened the doors.

Fresh, cold air rushed in, along with the smell of pine. I saw the stars and a half circle of moon and the trees with mist swirling around their tops.

Behind the surfboard was a plank that he used for a ramp; he rolled the little motorbike down easily.

"Just so you know," he said. "This place is supposed to be closed to traffic at night. Hardly anybody comes up here. So don't bother hoping you'll be found. I'll be back before you know it, three or four hours at the most."

He slid the plank back in and clicked off the lights. The doors slammed. The locks turned. The motorbike kicked over and grumbled as he revved it up.

I heard it go. I heard the deep, empty silence it left behind.

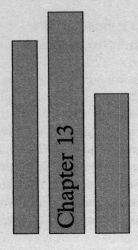

Chapter 13

I sucked in my cheeks, moved my jaw from side to side so many times it began to go numb, lifted my head, and shook the silk scarf down around my throat. Then I pulled in great gasps of the stuffy van air, thinking that I would never again take breathing for granted.

The dark surrounded me. No time to rest. Fred was on his way with the ransom note for Mom, and he'd said he'd be back before I knew it. No time to think of how Mom would feel when she got the note. I'd been through all that before. No need to think how it would be for me, if Fred got back before I escaped. I'd been through that in my dark imaginings, too.

My hope was clipped to my belt, hidden under the long bulk of the sweatshirt—Leah's Easi-Talkie.

The one thing he'd missed. But how could I get to it? If only he'd tied my hands in front instead of in back.

The first thing I had to do was get the light on.

I bent my knees, my feet against the floor, inching backward. When my head bumped the side of the van, I got my feet under me and edged up so I was standing with my shoulders against the wall. The light switch was to my left. I remembered it just behind the driver's seat. I moved my head in searching circles against the wall, hopping sideways, and there it was, the outline of the switch against my left cheek. I pushed up and the light went on.

Oh, man! Nothing was quite as bad when that silent darkness left. Bad still, but at least I could see.

Now I had to get to the Easi-Talkie. I plucked at my sweatshirt with my teeth, trying to get it raised, but each time I let go it fell again. Getting the sweatshirt up wasn't going to do any good anyway. I looked around and saw the surfboard lying on its rack, the fin sticking out in my direction, and I hopped over and pressed my stomach against it. I felt the fin's sharp point, dulled through the sweatshirt. It was below the bottom edge of the Easi-Talkie. I bent my knees, keeping the pressure hard, feeling the fin scrape up, stop at the bottom edge of the box. Come on, come on, I thought. Bring it with you, push the clip off the belt, over the turned down waistband of the shorts.

The fin slipped away, skidding up the side of the box, stabbing me under my chin. I was sweating and felt myself beginning to panic. "Don't hurry so much," I muttered. But how much time had I used up already? How much did I have left?

I made myself take a deep breath and count to ten. Outside a night bird sang, the trees sighed. I tried again.

I got the Easi-Talkie on the sixth try. It came loose from my belt and fell on my right foot. I eased it gently off onto the floor.

"Thank you, thank you, thank you," I said, though I wasn't sure who I was thanking.

I thumped myself down on the matting, banging my elbows hard, turned on my side, and felt behind me. There it was. Little by little I slid up the aerial. It seemed to take forever, holding the box with one hand, the fingers of my other hand slipping and sliding on the thin chrome. I had it.

I pushed the On button, moved the slide bar to Talk, rolled over to face it.

My mouth was so dry I had to lick my lips and swallow before I could speak. "WA6WXG," I croaked. "Calling WA6WXG." I rolled my back toward the box, pushed the bar to the Receive position and listened. Nothing. Leah would be asleep. It must be about two in the morning. She'd said she'd leave her big Yaesu open all the time, but how could she hear me calling if she was asleep? I turned back and tried again. "WA6WXG, come in. This is an emergency."

Nothing.

Hadn't Leah said once that the airways were open? Why didn't someone come in? Someone in Madagascar, or Timbuktu. Why didn't Pud come in? Maybe I should move the top button and put it on a different setting. That's what I'd do. I'd try one more time and if . . .

"This is WA6WXG," came the voice. "Come in."

Leah. I was so excited and so relieved that I skidded the Easi-Talkie away from me as I tried to push the bar up with my chin.

"Don't go, Leah. Wait. Don't go," I said frantically, talking to myself, begging. I got it—slid up the bar.

"Leah. It's Andy." It didn't matter anymore if I said my name. Let the whole world hear it. Let the whole world come and save me. "Listen . . . I've been kidnapped. The guy's name is Fred. He works at the hotel. He caught me in the room. My hands and feet are tied and I'm locked in his van. It's blue. It says Surf Rider on the side. The windows are blacked out and there are white squiggles on the roof. We're about an hour and a half from the hotel. I don't know where but it's high up and there are pine trees. We went across the Golden Gate Bridge to somewhere that's closed to cars at night, a park maybe. Leah, you have to hurry. Fred could come back anytime. Call Mom and Paul. Get the police. But come back, OK? Please come back." I didn't even care if she heard me crying. It didn't matter.

I slid the bar so I could hear her.

"Oh, Andy! I'm going. But I'll be right back. Hold on. Just hold on."

I lay then with my face to the Easi-Talkie, waiting, crying some more, shrugging my face into Fred's silk scarf to wipe the bubbles from my nose and eyes. It was taking her forever. What was she doing? I should have told her to hurry. Hurry, Leah! I'm trying to hold on. Please hurry!

"Andy?"

"I'm still here. I wish I wasn't."

"Andy. I called your mom. She's getting the police right away. They'll find you. They will. Here's my dad."

"Can you remember anything else that might help the police, Andy? Anything?" Leah's dad asked.

It took every bit of strength that I had left to push the talk bar.

"Nothing." And then I did remember something really important. "Oh—Fred's on a motorbike, a small one, red. I should have gotten the number, but I didn't."

"You hold on, son. The police will find you."

And then it was Leah's mom's voice. "Your mother is going with the police in one of their cars,

Andy. She says to tell you she loves you. She loves you very much."

I know, I said. But only to myself.

Leah was back. "Andy? Do you want to talk? We can talk while you wait for them to get to you."

Wait for *who* to get to me, I thought. Fred could come back anytime. He could move the van. They might never find me. But I didn't say any of that, either.

"I feel rotten," I told Leah. "A lot of this is my own fault."

"Yeah," Leah agreed.

Trust Leah. Wouldn't you think that since I'd been kidnapped and was waiting to maybe be *murdered* she'd be nicer?

"You have been acting really dumb ever since Paul," she said, and I lay, knowing she was right, listening to the silence and wondering if I'd ever tell her about that first kidnap note, the one I'd written myself. I'd have to. She'd call me worse than dumb then, all right. I could just hear her. "Have you learned your lesson?" she'd ask. "What lesson?" "You know, not to be jealous." "Oh, clam up," I'd say and then she'd probably start to tell me some unbelievably wonderful story about Pud. Leah just doesn't have any tact.

"Andy?" she asked. "Are you still there?"

Where did she *think* I'd be?

"The police want to talk to you."

And then the cops came on Leah's radio and they asked me all sorts of questions, including the same thing Leah's dad asked about—if I knew anything more—and I said I didn't. But then they asked me to describe Fred and what he was wearing and if he had a helmet, and I told them. I even remembered the chains on his boots. They said that was very helpful and for me to stay where I was and to keep real close to the Easi-Talkie. They'd be there, on the other end. What was it with everyone thinking I was going somewhere?

"They say it's OK if I keep talking to you," Leah told me. "If that's all right with you."

"Yes," I said. "Please."

"How about if I read to you? Reading's great to keep your mind off . . . you know, problems."

I couldn't seem to make the effort to push the bar anymore so I didn't answer. I imagined her going to the messy bookcase beside her desk, pulling out a book.

"Man!" she said. "Parker's going to be sorry he missed out on all this. He's sleeping over at Grandma's." I thought I heard pages turning and then she said, "Ready? '*Mr. Sherlock Holmes, who was usually very late in the mornings,* . . .' "

It was our favorite . . . *The Hound of the Baskervilles.*

I lay on my side in the dim van light, half listening to the story that I almost knew by heart, listening through it for the growl of Fred's motorbike coming back. What would he do to me if he came? But maybe they'd caught him already? No, they'd tell me, wouldn't they, when they did?

" ' "Really, Watson, you excel yourself," said Holmes.' "

I made the effort and pushed the bar. "Leah? Ask the police to tell me if they catch Fred. Ask them to tell me the very second they know themselves, OK?"

I heard the faint murmur as she talked to them. "They say they will. The absolute second."

What would they do to Fred if they caught him? Jail for sure. Maybe worse. It was so cold in the van that I was shivering. My hands and feet were numb. The smell of Fred's scarf made me want to barf.

Leah's voice read on and on.

Fred had said he'd run away when he was my age. What was he like then? I had the feeling he was the kind of person who got into bad trouble without meaning to. Things would get away from him and grow and grow. I was shivering even more now. Look how all this got away from me.

I love *The Hound of the Baskervilles*, but even so, and even though I was freezing, I think I fell asleep.

It was the loud chug-chug of an engine that woke me. I remembered right away where I was and why and my heart bumped with terror. Fred was back.

On the Easi-Talkie Leah was still reading.

126

I fumbled for the bar. Oh, no. He was back and . . .

My hands were numb. I couldn't even find the box. Why hadn't I switched off the light? Fred would see it and he'd know something was wrong. I should have hidden the Easi-Talkie, too. I rolled myself face-down and felt it underneath me and then I realized that the chug-chug sound wasn't outside at all, it was above the van . . . it was in the sky . . . and through the corner of the window I could see a searchlight circling.

"A helicopter," I yelled, and I tried to stand, but somehow I couldn't get my knees to bend anymore. From under my stomach, Leah's muffled voice said, "'*Chapter Three. The Problem. I confess that at these words a shudder passed through me.*'"

I rolled off the Easi-Talkie, got my chin on the bar and pushed. "Leah," I whispered. "I think the police are here. I think I'm saved. Leah, thanks."

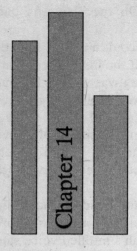

Chapter 14

The doors of the van were pried open. Police officers jumped in beside me, four or five of them, enough to fill the whole space. A policewoman was trying to untie my wrists, and a man in a dark red windbreaker cut the rope around my ankles. In the end he had to cut the wrist ropes, too. The policewoman rubbed my arms and legs and helped me get up.

"Are you OK, Andy?"

"I think so," I said, though I hurt so much I could hardly stand. Through the open doors I saw more cars driving up, their headlights cutting the darkness, tires crunching noisily on fallen pine cones. The helicopter circled low above us.

The officer who'd cut the ropes smiled down at

me. "You did really well, Andy. There weren't that many woodsy places he could hide a van over here, less than a couple of hours from the city. The chopper picked up on that roof design fast."

It hadn't seemed that fast to me. Someone gave me a cup of hot chocolate from a thermos. I'd never tasted anything so good.

"Did you find Fred yet?" I asked. "You know, the guy who brought me here?"

"Not yet. But we will."

"Is my mom coming?"

"She's waiting for you at the station, Andy. But look, here's your dad."

"My *dad?*" I couldn't believe it. How did my dad get here so fast? It would have taken him all night to fly from England.

And then I saw Paul Paws getting out of a police car that had just cruised to a stop, Paul Paws running toward the van.

"It's my stepdad," I told the officer.

"Oh, yeah? Well, sometimes they're just as good as the real thing. Sometimes better."

Paul Paws helped me down and held my arms as he crouched in front of me. "Are you all right, Andy?" His voice and his mustache were both quivering.

"I think so," I said.

The officer who'd been in the car with him ran up, too, and stood grinning at us. "I sure like a happy ending," he said. "Your poor, tired old dad here has been cruising with us for two nights, helping us try to find you."

Paul Paws stood up and ran his hands through his hair. For the first time I noticed how awful he looked, with a black stubble of beard and his eyes all droopy. I probably didn't look too great myself, though I was minus the beard.

"Well, I got to be one of the first to hear the chopper had found you," Paul Paws said. "That made it all worthwhile."

I didn't know what to say, so I just said, "Well, thanks."

"Why don't you and your dad hop in the car there, and we'll be on our way," the officer said. "We'll need to talk to you at the station, Andy, before you go home."

My stomach did a nervous flip. My poor stomach had been flipping so much tonight that I doubted it would ever recover. "I did a lot of bad things myself," I said, hoping to prepare them a bit for what I'd have to tell them. "I think I put some of these kidnapping ideas into Fred's head."

"Well, I doubt if we'll prosecute you," the officer said and then he added, "Of course, you never can tell." But his smile was kind. I tried to hold onto that smile for comfort. They truly wouldn't prosecute a kid, would they? One who'd been kidnapped and all.

The police were putting yellow tapes around the

van now, and there were two officers inside examining all the stuff in back.

"Wait," I said. "I have to take Leah's Easi-Talkie."

"It'll be safe. We don't want to disturb anything."

"It better be safe," I said. "If it isn't, Leah will kill me. That Easi-Talkie was for Christmas and her birthday, too."

"We'll take care of it."

It was a nice thought that I'd be seeing Leah again after all. I sure would have missed her in England.

I looked back at the van once as we drove away, and I began shivering again. Paul put his arm loosely around my shoulders.

It was almost morning. I don't think it was raining much, but the driver had to keep the windshield wipers on, beating back and forth as we drove.

"Did Mom call Dad?" I asked, and Paul said, "Yes, and I'm sure he would have come, Andy. But she couldn't reach him."

"I couldn't, either. It's real hard to reach him." I heard what I'd said, and I knew it had always been true about Dad. I was wishing, too, that I hadn't brought up the subject, because Paul had been so nice, looking for me and not even sleeping, and here I was talking about Dad again. Seems like I'm always talking about Dad when Paul's around.

"I'm sorry I gave you and Mom all this trouble,

and I'm sorry I took your money. Maybe they'll get it back when they find Fred."

"Maybe."

"I looked at the stars a lot," I said. "There was a telescope. I really like the stars."

Paul smiled. "Good."

His arm tightened around my shoulders, and I felt a great swoop of relief. He understood about the stars.

We were driving across the Golden Gate now, fog billowing around us, San Francisco still sleeping on the other side of the bay. The city streets were damp and gray and empty. Two taxi drivers stood by their cabs, their jacket collars up, drinking from paper cups. It was cold.

"I hope they got Barnstable back," I said.

"Barnstable?"

"Just a ginger cat I know," I said.

We passed the Countess International, the lighted elevators resting at ground level, the glass towers dull and blank. I pictured the suite, Mamie's flowers, the peaches in the fruit bowl, and I thought I'd be able to close my eyes and remember all of it, always. And then we were pulling up in front of the police station.

The two officers got out of the car and one said, "Here we go, Andy."

I was scared all of a sudden. Part of this was over, but another part was just beginning.

"You'll come, too, won't you, Paul?" I asked.

"Yes," Paul said.

"I did a lot of bad things," I muttered, and Paul said, "We love you."

And then the door of the police station opened, and there was Mom. Even from here, even in the dull light of morning, I could see the diamond bow glittering in her hair.